WIDOW'S MIGHT

BOOK THREE OF THE
CLAN NOVEL:TREMERE TRILOGY

By Eric Griffin

www.worldofdarkness.com

Acknowledgments

I would like to thank Stewart Wieck—publisher, editor and friend—for his faith and support from the beginning, Philippe Boulle for his tenacity and guidance, Anna Branscome for her herculean efforts in rendering my freestyle Latin (not to mention, Victorian prose) into more comprehensible form, and of course, my wife Victoria for ten wonderful years of her beauty, company, patience, grace and love.

—*Preludes*, T.S. Eliot

Chapter One
Widow's Weeds

At the end of the incline, Antigone saw a dark form dangling from the railing. More accurately, it seemed to be pinned between the tangle of walk and railing, and struggling to free itself. The Bonespeaker.

He hung head-downwards, suspended and inverted. The walk here had sagged so low that the fall would not have been anything to speak of, certainly no more than ten feet. Below, Antigone could see a form stalking towards them out of the darkness.

She froze, expecting more gunshots.

For the first time this evening, she was pleasantly disappointed. In the dim light from the window, the approaching figure gradually took on the familiar shape of Felton.

His visage was grim. Most of the flesh of his forehead had been clawed away, apparently in the effort to extract the bullet. It did not look as if the operation had been a success. Much of his face was covered with angry-looking flash burns. He walked with a decided limp, his pants leg shredded by a veritable strafing run of bullet wounds.

Without ever taking his eyes from the Bonespeaker, Felton let the detonator drop to the floor. He came three paces closer, stooped and picked up a large-caliber automatic pistol that had fallen from the Speaker's grip when the explosive charge went off below him. In Felton's other hand, he held a bloody straight razor.

Antigone hardly recognized it. Like Felton, the blade had not suffered the rain of bullets gracefully. It was badly bent, nicked, its handle shattered.

Felton raised the gun and leveled it at the Bonespeaker's head. From these close quarters, Antigone could see that the pistol looked to have escaped in much better condition. Not surprising as it had been on the giving, rather than the receiving, end of most of the carnage. "Stand clear, Ms. Baines. He's mine. He's got it coming to him. And I'm going to finish this, right now."

"Nope," she replied, planting one foot firmly on the Bonespeaker's sternum and digging in. "Think a minute, Mr. Felton. You kill him now and we're never going to find out who set me—who set *you* up."

The change of emphasis was not lost on him. Slowly, the pistol lowered to his side. "So that's what this is all about. I should have known better than to think that the damned Tremere would just help me out without having some personal stake in the outcome."

The Bonespeaker laughed softly. The sound bubbled out of him like a spring. There didn't seem to be any end to it. "The Tremere? A personal stake in this matter... Our Ms. Baines really has kept you in the dark, then, hasn't she?"

"And you, shut the hell up!" Felton yelled. "I'm serious, I'm not going to tell you again. You think I'm going to hold back because *she* might get caught in the line of fire? You're fooling yourself. So, shut up already!"

Antigone put the whole of her weight upon her one heel. It ground all the air out of the Bonespeaker and the laughter with it. "Felton..." she interrupted gently.

"What?"

"I'd like to get out of here, preferably before the police arrive. We can't go anywhere until I get a certain answer out of this man. I would already have gotten it, if you hadn't barged in here five minutes early and nearly gotten the both of us killed in the bargain. So if you would just hold off on killing this bastard for a minute, I think we can all get what we want. Okay?"

"Did I mention you're starting to piss me off?" he said. "Now I remember why I work alone. The sooner we get this over with, the better, as far as I'm concerned. Here you go. Ask away. I'll be right here if you need me." He tossed the razor up to her.

She caught it, was about to make an angry retort and then thought better of it. Instead, she stooped over the Bonespeaker and held up the blade for his inspection.

"Okay, B.S. It's all up to you now. We can kill you, or we can cut you first and then kill you. I want to know why. That's all. Why you went to all the trouble to set me up. I already know why you blew up the building. To take down the prince. That's what this whole damned takeover of the Conventicle is about, isn't it? But what I want to know is, why me?" The blade nuzzled up against his throat.

"You still don't understand, do you?" he said, his voice rasping through the stark white avian mask. "Now put the knife down and think for a minute. I didn't blow up the building."

Below, Felton cursed and began pacing.

"Like hell you didn't!" Antigone shouted directly into the Bonespeaker's face. With an angry slash, she wrenched the blade down and around in a tight arc.

His head fell back, dangling over the abyss as if suddenly deprived of all visible means of support. A frail gurgle bubbled up through the mask as he clutched at his throat.

Felton, standing exactly below him, met his eyes. He could see the fear and confusion there as the Bonespeaker's hands came away, not covered with his spilling lifeblood, but perfectly dry.

"Oh shit." Felton said sadly, shaking his head. "Now you're in for it. You know what that is, don't you? It's blood magic. Thaumaturgy. I've seen her perform this little trick before and it's pretty gruesome. My advice to you is to answer the lady's questions as quickly and accurately as possible. You should've stuck by me, pal. I would have just shot you."

Antigone balled a fist into the front of the Bonespeaker's robes and hauled him back to a sitting position. "Who blew up the damned building?" she demanded.

"I… don't… know."

"Damn, he sounds bad," Felton said. "Like his vocal chords have been severed or something."

"Shut up, Felton," she barked. Her eyes never left the bone-white mask. "You. Listen to me. Was it any of our folks? Anybody in the Conventicle?" Antigone was thinking of the dark woman who had picked up the redress—who had set off the explosion at the high school in attempt to kill or silence Johanus.

"No," he rasped. He tried to clear his throat, coughed and spat bloody phlegm down over the side of the swaying walkway. Felton scowled up at him. The Bonespeaker tested his voice again and it sounded steadier this time. "If you had any idea what you have blundered into, Ms. Baines, you would not be so eager to cut yourself off from all of your allies. Yet you systematically alienate yourself from anyone who might protect you—from the Pyramid, from the Conventicle, and now even from your last fawning supporter, poor deluded Mr. Felton."

"Just waste this bastard," Felton said. "He doesn't know anything."

"I'm a big girl," Antigone answered the Bonespeaker. "I can watch my own back. So how about you tell me why you, my so-called benefactor, set me up? You knew the building was going to blow. You even knew when it was going to happen. And you arranged things so that I would be there to take the fall. Why?"

The Bonespeaker laughed quietly. "You don't know. You really don't know. And I thought you were just stringing our Mr. Felton here along. You don't see why it would alarm me to have another Tremere infiltrating the Conventicle at this point? *Especially* a member of the chantry security team."

"What the hell do you mean 'another' Tremere?" Antigone asked. "Jeezus, there are other novices from the chantry inside the Conventicle and you didn't even see fit to tell me?!"

Jervais shook his head. "Of course there is another. And your presence—not to mention your determination to force your way up through the ranks—put the infiltrator in a rather tenuous position."

"I need a name," Antigone growled.

"And you'll have one," he said. "If you will see reason. Surely you realize that you cannot go back to the chantry now. Not even Helena could protect you. So where will you go? Your only hope is the Conventicle. I can hide you from the prince and the Pyramid. We will lead the Conventicle through this crisis together. I am willing to make a blood compact with you."

"You tried to kill me before," she reminded him.

"No, I tried to get you out of harm's way. To get you to leave the city. I knew that if you kept on the way you were going, you would get us both killed. I couldn't let you jeopardize all I have built here. The Conventicle is my House, Antigone. My chantry, if you will. You of all people can appreciate what that means. I am offering you the protection of my House."

She shook her head. "It's too late for all that now. You should have offered me that weeks ago, before this whole mess started. Then none of this would have happened. And you wouldn't be about to die. Now, one last time, how did you know the Empire State Building was going to be blown up? I need a name."

"If I tell you that, we're both as good as dead."

"You're already as good as dead, and I'm willing to take the chance. Now tell me! Who tipped you off?"

The Bonespeaker fidgeted uncomfortably. "His name is Graves. Adam Graves. He's..."

Antigone knew very well who he was. His face had been plastered all over the news of late.

"Lying son of a bitch," Felton muttered from below. "I've seen that guy, Graves. On TV. *Daytime* TV. He's not even one of us."

Antigone ignored Felton's outburst. She knew that if the Bonespeaker were lying, she'd know about it immediately.

"Look, you remember the last time we met?" When you sent me out to kill Felton...?" she said.

"What the fuck?" Felton demanded indignantly from below.

The Bonespeaker shifted uneasily. He hesitated; he cleared his throat. Antigone shook him by the collar. "Do you?!"

"Yes, certainly. I..."

A hot wave of blood slapped across Antigone's face. Felton stepped back hastily, cursing. The Bonespeaker's back arched sharply and then he went limp in her grasp.

"Damn it." She brought her fist down, pounding on his chest, and then pushed him sharply away. His head swung down below the level of the walk. A cascade of blood pattered to the floor from the gaping slit in his throat.

"Oh, that was great," Felton said, wiping at the splattered blood on the front of his shirt. "Very effective. Can we get out of here now? Or would you like to cross-examine the corpse?"

"You go ahead," she said, clenching her teeth over an angry retort. "I've got one more question to ask him."

Felton snorted in disgust. "You're crazy, you know that, right? This guy's done answering. He's... Never mind. It's not worth it. You're not listening anyway. Look, I'll wait downstairs for you, if you want me to. I figure, you did help me out when I had nowhere else to go. And you came back for me, back at the chantry, and pulled me out of that inferno. And even if your motives weren't entirely altruistic, you deserve something. At least for somebody to give you a heads-up before the cops bust in."

His unanticipated offer brought her up short. "That's very considerate of you, Mr. Felton. I'll see you back in the warrens then."

"Jeez, you are crazy. I'll see you around, Blackbird."

Antigone looked after him until she heard the street door bang shut. Then she tugged the limp body back up onto the remains of the walk. The chalk-white mask was streaked with blood. The pattern caught her by surprise. Like the counter-intuitive course of the Nile, the ruby lines ran *upwards*, south to north—a side effect of the body's dangling upside down.

Antigone stared at the alien bird-like features a long while. Felton's words of a week before kept running through her mind: *All of the bosses are interchangeable.*

The Bonespeaker had failed the razor's test. He had been caught out in a lie. *But it wasn't a lie!* Antigone silently raged. He had merely admitted to sending her to kill Felton at their last meeting. Or had he?

The troubling thought struck her, remembering how the Bonespeaker had hesitated when she had put the question to him. *What if that hadn't been their last meeting?*

With growing apprehension, she hooked her fingers under the edge of the mask and pulled. It refused to come away, as if the surface tension of the blood film had sealed it to his face. She tugged harder, but to no avail.

Frustrated, she grabbed the object that was closest to hand. Occam's Razor. Inserting the blade through one eyehole, she insinuated it between the mask and the underlying flesh. Then she bore down hard, using the razor as a lever.

The blade bent nearly double. Antigone sat back on her heels, staring at it in open incredulity. Instead of a straight razor, she found that she clutched a long black feather. She recognized it instantly—the Feather of Ma'at. The jackal god's standard for taking the measure of the dead. She remembered his parting words to her—about the inherent interchangeability of the symbols of truth. About his allowing her to go back and be judged by the symbols of her own people—by the standards of her own peers.

At the time, she had been afraid that he had meant she would be returned to face the inquisition of the astors. But it seemed that the Laughing Guardian of the Dead had picked out three very different judges for her from among her brothers and sisters of the Tremere Pyramid.

She thought back to her encounters with Johanus, with Jervais, with Helena—and of the trials and the accusations that each had laid before her. Some of them she had met well, with honesty and compassion. Others, not so well.

She hadn't found any easy redemptions, nor earned the absolution of even a single one of her tribunal of judges. If this feather was a summons from the Jackal, a sign that her time here was drawing to a close, she was afraid that she did not have anything to show him for her sojourn here. Even with his second chance, she hadn't managed to do any better this time around. She had tried to help some people; she had hurt others. She had shed blood and drawn blood. She had sought after the truth, and she had been willing to bend the truth to do so.

So where did that leave her in the final reckoning? She feared that if she were to face the Jackal's golden scales again now, the verdict would be no different than it had been before.

She was no monster, although her very existence had become monstrous. She was certainly no saint, although she acutely felt the weight of the twin burdens of truth and compassion. She knew she had been given gifts both beautiful and terrifying — and that because of them, she would be held accountable to a higher standard.

She was empty of all desire now, but also curiously free of all fear. There was nothing left to her but the inevitable. She moved a hand through time, and eternity danced upon her fingertips.

Confidently, she reached out and laid the feather on her side of the balances, for a change.

Antigone laid the Feather of Ma'at gently across the sharp avian contours of the Bonespeaker's mask, like a shroud drawn up to cover the staring eyes of the deceased.

The skeletal bird mask cracked neatly in two vertically, the pieces falling away to either side.

Antigone glanced only briefly at the familiar face that was revealed there. The face of one of her judges — the one she had most failed.

Jervais.

She had abandoned Johanus to deal with the aftermath of the explosion alone. To drag the bodies from the wreckage, to tend the wounded and dying, and to hide the evidence from the authorities.

She had left Helena to the mercy of the astors. To bear the brunt of their inquisition, to comfort the novices, to try to hold the crumbling chantry together by sheer force of will.

But Jervais she had failed most of all.

Carefully, Antigone gathered up the halves of the mask. She cradled them in her arms, like broken eggshells, as she descended from the walk.

A gunshot sounded in the street outside. *Felton's warning,* she thought. Already she could pick out the wail of sirens drawing closer. She knew she must hurry now. But still she stood, rooted to the spot, listening. Waiting to be called back to face the final judgment. In the baying of the sirens, she thought she could detect the faint mocking laughter of the Jackal.

He was laughing at her. It was not until that moment that Antigone realized that she was not going to be suddenly whisked away. She could no longer dance the fine line between the living and the dead and walk away unscathed. If she were going to walk away from this room at all, she would have to take responsibility for her own redemption. To become her own judge—self-accused and, hopefully, self-vindicating.

Slowly, she raised the shattered mask to her face and, for the first time, looked out through the impassive avian eyes of the Bonespeaker.

Chapter Two
A Thousand Years Deep

Sturbridge's memories of her previous trip to the Fatherhouse were disjointed, almost feverish. The edifice had a weight of history and tradition about it unlike anything she had experienced anywhere else. It was simply too much to take in at once. Just being here felt a little like drowning. Of being thrown into a dark well, a thousand years deep—while yoked to a great pyramid-shaped stone.

The walls of the old manse had once, no doubt, been white, pristine. But the centuries of dark rites enacted within them had taken their toll on the place. The antique hand-painted wallpaper had turned a uniform dark sepia, as if it had soaked up some sanguine essence from the rivers of life that had been spilled here.

Sturbridge passively allowed herself to be guided through the half-familiar galleries and balustrades. She peered down upon the formal ballrooms and conservatories, her eyes and ears filled with the ethereal afterimages of legendary performances of bygone eras. Performances that had risen to greatness unaware of—and actually masking—the wailing of the afflicted coming from the labyrinthine cellars.

Sturbridge could feel eyes upon her as well. Luminaries of her order regarded her curiously at her passing. They whispered behind their hands at the sight of anyone in these halls—much less a lady of such regal bearing—attired in the humble black robes of the novitiate. The widow's weeds were tolerated here, but it was expected that they should be relegated to the churchyard, not ushered within the halls of power.

But there were other eyes here as well. Eyes more penetrating and more vigilant. Sturbridge could feel their scrutiny like groping hands. Ghosts, daemons, guardian spirits and gargoyles frowned down at her from every cornice, capital, buttress and rainspout. The stunted servitors of the old manse craned down towards her as she passed, hungering.

Sturbridge could not evade the need in their eyes, the silent pleading. She closed her own eyelids against them, only to find herself confronted by other faces. Faces of the twisted and the lost, rising up to greet their counterparts. From somewhere deep within her, eyes as round and bright as moons broke from the surface of dark waters and peered curiously out at these other victims, those still clinging to the world of the living. Trapped on the far side of the chill, rippling mirror.

She could feel Dorfman's hand upon her elbow, but there was no comfort in it, no warmth. At times it seemed that she could barely see him through the haze of rippling victims that pressed her from all sides. From without and from within.

"It was a mistake to come here," she said with certainty. "You see how they titter? How they talk behind their hands? The words of my accusers have proceeded us. They have already hardened their hearts against us."

"It's all right," Dorfman said, his voice tight and pitched low. "Ignore them. The only person we've got to convince is Meerlinda. We talk to her, we find out what we need to know, and then we're out of here."

"You still think they're just going to let us say our piece and walk out of here alive?" Sturbridge demanded. "Look around you. Do these strike you as the kind of folks who suffer any kind of shake-up gracefully?"

"Look, it's been a long night," Dorfman said. "We could both use some rest. Tomorrow night we'll see Meerlinda. We will make her understand. I've got everything taken care of."

"Oh, you do not." But she smiled at his attempt. They walked for a while in silence, but a dim sense of foreboding was growing in her, fueled by the whispers of this old manse and its many victims. "This place is so cold, so empty. Can you feel it? It is an overwhelming sense of… absence. He is not here," she said with sudden certainty.

"What are you talking about? Who's not here?"

Sturbridge's tone was very calm, conversational, belying the growing horror of her realization.

"He has abandoned this place, shrugged it off like an old and ill-fitting garment. Shed it like a skin. Can't you see, Peter? He has freed himself from the Children, from their mute reproaches. He has freed himself of his childer, from the ceaseless feuding and bickering of his blood descendants. And now there is no telling what he might be capable of. How can they stay here? How can they stand it? Going through the same sad pantomime, night after night. Pretending that nothing has happened. These harlequin magi. These hollow men. Oh, it was foolish to have ever come here."

Dorfman smiled. A radiant, authentic smile. Something about it, its tangibility, broke in upon her dark musings and pulled her back away from the brink of that dark inner well. It seemed to encompass everything about them at once—the inspiration that breathed from the very architecture, the anchoring weight of history and tradition, the company of keen centuries-old intellects. And the certainty, the surety he could feel in his very blood, that this was home.

"I was just thinking," he confessed, "that I was a fool ever to have left it."

Chapter Three
A Grave Matter

Antigone checked the address a third time. Yes, this was it. The apartment building was modest by New York standards, a mere seven stories. But it was well-kept, and that counted for something. It had sprouted up from good soil—a solid neighborhood—and everything looked clean and in good repair from the street. There was something about the place, however, that just didn't feel right. Something Antigone couldn't quite put her finger on.

The problem nibbled away at the back of her mind as she ascended the steps and pushed through the front doors, which were not locked, even at this hour. This oversight set off another faint warning bell for her. She glanced at the orderly columns of mailboxes and door buzzers in the entrance hall, none of them labeled with anything more revealing than an apartment number. It was difficult for her to credit that there was not at least one curling yellowed strip of notebook paper clumsily taped up under a doorbell. Not a single hastily hand-scribbled name.

The hallway stretched away in front of her, clean and orderly, free of the detritus she had come to associate with apartment-house corridors. No chained-up bicycles. No broken-down appliances waiting to be carted off to the basement. Not even the mandatory empty metal bracket where the fire extinguisher had hung before someone had made off with it. She stopped dead in the middle of the hall, shaking her head in disbelief, and just listened. Nothing.

Antigone tried to keep her mind off that silence as she waited for the elevator. No sound of children or loud music or even the soporific buzz of late-night television humming down the hall. It wasn't right. The entire building felt hollow, empty. Devoid of life.

As the elevator doors slid shut, Antigone tried to recall everything she knew about this Adam Graves. Even she had to admit it amounted to very little. She knew he was some bigwig at Cyanight Entertainment, a splashy national Internet service provider. She knew that he worked in public relations. She had seen him on the news in connection with the recent bombing at the Empire State Building — something about his company yanking a controversial ad in light of the recent disaster.

Most importantly, she knew that, just before Jervais died, he had identified Graves as the person who had tipped him off about the bombing at the Empire State Building.

Antigone still didn't see how it all added up. Why would some dotcom publicity wank be privy to advance information on a terrorist strike? It didn't exactly fit the job description. Furthermore, she could have sworn that a number of those televised interview segments had been shot outside, in broad daylight, which seemed to point pretty clearly to the fact that Mr. Graves was not one of her kind. Undying nocturnal predators and sunlight just didn't mix.

If Graves was responsible, that seemed to cut the legs out from under any conspiracy theories about the bombing being an assassination attempt. The vast majority of the city's nineteen million diurnal residents remained blissfully unaware of the existence of their benighted counterparts. It would be a stretch to think that a "mere mortal" would even know that New York City had a vampiric prince. Even less plausible was the idea that some hypothetical mortal assassin would have either motive or opportunity to take a shot at the elusive Nosferatu prince. Calebros did not exactly advertise his whereabouts. Antigone herself had been in mortal danger during the uncertain weeks when she was compiling information for the hit on Emmet, the prince's right-hand man. And Antigone had more than a passing familiarity with the ways of the undying, as well as intelligence gathering.

So who the hell was this Adam Graves, and where did he come into this mess? Antigone didn't know yet, but she'd come here tonight to find some answers.

With the resources of the chantry suddenly jerked out from under her, Antigone had had to satisfy herself with going into this confrontation on a minimum of prep work. She had done a bit of background checking on Mr. Graves, but nothing really jumped out at her. He hailed from Indiana, went to school at Yale and took a degree in business communications. He was married for six years, divorced. The two kids lived with their mom somewhere in the Carolinas. Graves had lived here, in an apartment on the seventh floor, for the last year and a half. The apartment—like most of the apartments on the seventh floor—was owned by the company.

As the elevator doors chimed open, Antigone was immediately aware that there was something amiss. It was something in the furtive shuffle of human life that she could sense hovering just beyond bolted apartment doors. She could almost see the heat of their bodies, leaning in close, pressing ears to doors. She could pick out the stutter-step of agitated pulses and, in at least one instance, the ominous click of a pistol's hammer drawing back.

There was a barely perceptible flutter of eyes to peepholes. Yes, Antigone could recognize the signs. This was not a bad neighborhood. Quite the opposite. But these people had been shaken recently. They had been through some ordeal. Judging from the unique combination of speed and timidity with which they answered the sound of the elevator's chime, Antigone knew that the residents were none too anxious for a repeat performance.

She had an unsettling presentiment, as if she already knew what she must find, even before she turned the elbow of the corridor. Antigone didn't need to read off the burnished brass door numbers to tell which one belonged to the mysterious Mr. Graves. The yellow police tape with its bold black lettering proclaimed it loud and clear: *Police Line Do Not Cross.*

The dangling adhesive strips crisscrossed the doorway from corner to corner, forming a huge X. A polished chrome ball-lock swallowed the doorknob, to prevent entry even by someone who had the apartment key.

Her apprehensions realized, Antigone deflated. She paused before the door, uncertain of her next move, straining to pick up any telltale signs of activity beyond the portal. She didn't really expect any. The scene said all too clearly that the authorities had already been here and moved on.

Well, there was no help for it now. Striking what she hoped was an official-looking stance, she squared her shoulders and took the ball-lock firmly in hand. She gave it a good rattle that she hoped any eavesdroppers up and down the hall would mistake for the fumbling of a key in the lock. She cursed once for good measure. Cops always cursed when they were alone. It was one thing on which all the TV dramas concurred.

The jamb splintered and the latch sprang from its moorings with a bit more noise than she would have liked. But the operation had been accomplished with so little outward display of physical violence—and Antigone's slight build hardly looked equal to smashing down a door to begin with—that she thought it would do.

She ducked around and through the police tape and entered Graves' apartment, pushing the door back behind her. She couldn't close or latch it again, but her object wasn't to keep people out, only to dissuade the idly curious.

She followed the smell of blood, spilled liquor and spent gunpowder through the living room. She worked her way through in darkness, trusting in her keen senses and the inch of moonlight creeping from beneath the pull-down window shade to show her what she needed to see. There were still-wet rings on the table nearest the sofa, telltale signs of a bottle and a glass. Perhaps two glasses, it was hard to tell. The police, however, seemed to have commandeered the entire lot as evidence. Along with everything else that wasn't nailed down.

One corner of the living room doubled as an office and the desk was so free of clutter that Antigone had a hard time believing that this had been the way that Graves would have left it at the end of a workday. Either Mr. Graves had been a bit anal retentive, or his papers—like his Rolodex, his appointment book, and even the laptop whose empty docking station gaped like an open wound—had gone the way of the bottle. Police evidence.

She followed the unmistakable scent of blood back through an unused dining room. Feeling safer here from prying eyes from the corridor, Antigone drew back the drapes. In the sudden influx of moonlight, she could see the fine layer of dust that had settled into the hollow of each crystal wineglass. Obviously the table stayed set for decorative rather than functional reasons. A quick check revealed that one of the place settings, the one nearest the doorway to the living room, was missing both its wine and water glasses.

Antigone let the drapes fall back into place. Doors off the dining room led to a kitchen, two bedrooms and a bath. Not even bothering to peek into the other rooms, she went straight for the bath. The room was cramped, stuffy, but the air inside was cool. Maybe it was the heavy cloying odor that made it seem so claustrophobic. Antigone stepped in and pushed the door closed behind her using only one fingertip, instinctively shying away from contact with its surface. Only when the door had clicked closed did she flip on the light switch.

The room blazed to life; a row of spherical light globes ran the entire length of one wall, above the mirror. They gave off a ruddy-tinged light that cast an unhealthy glow over the room. The clean-up crew, no doubt working on a tight timetable, had managed to wipe away the majority of the blood and spattered gore. But the light fixtures—along with most of the left-hand wall, the door and parts of the ceiling—still bore the signs of the bloody deed that had been committed here.

Antigone wondered, idly, if there had been a note. Even if there had been, she knew, it wouldn't do her any good. New York's Finest would certainly not have left such a keepsake lying around.

She imagined there must have been something to throw suspicion over the affair, though, or the police would not have bothered to cart off so much of the detritus of Graves' daily life. There was never any real investigation of a suicide. And it was hardly worth the effort of poring over some poor stiff's computer files unless you suspected that he had had his hand in something not quite aboveboard.

But where did that leave her? Antigone just stood and stared at herself in the blood-flecked mirror. Graves had been Antigone's best—and last—lead. And now he was just another dead end.

Chapter Four
Honor Guard

The novice led Sturbridge down through the labyrinthine corridors with an air of wounded dignity. He had not quite balked when the castellan, Istavan, had entrusted the newcomer to his care. He understood that the tradition of guest-rite demanded that a visitor be formally escorted to her quarters, regardless of her station. But Gerard was certainly not accustomed to waiting upon mere novices—especially those who were still unblooded. He had immediately resolved to free himself of this unasked-for burden at the earliest opportunity.

He held himself erect and aloof, glaring at the other clansmen they chanced to meet, as if daring them to say anything. Anything at all. It was clear that Sturbridge's "honor guard" was anything but honored.

Sturbridge studied him in silence as he swept ahead of her, huffing to himself. Despite his pampered look—the coifed hair, the rich layers of silken finery that bore little resemblance to the coarse homespun novice robes of Sturbridge's own chantry—there was something lean and hungry about the man. Something that even the affected manners and excesses of this court could not quite cover. It was like catching sight of a skeletal hand peeking from an elegantly embroidered sleeve. In this case, a sleeve cuffed with silver.

The silver insignia at the wrist marked her escort as a novice of the third circle. Sturbridge had more than a passing familiarity with the breaking-in of novices. The first three circles of the novitiate she always thought of as the "ropes course." The neophytes of the first circle had to be individually and painstakingly shown the ropes. The apprentices of the second circle thought they knew everything, of course. And it always came as such a great surprise to them to discover that they really only knew enough of the ropes to hang themselves. It was the novices that managed to survive to the third circle, however, that were truly dangerous. These petty tyrants knew the ropes well enough that they could employ them in the hanging of others. And they would do so with shockingly slight provocation.

The third circles often took great pleasure at lording it over their juniors. Sturbridge had found it best to conceal from them the very existence of the fourth circle for as long as possible. The revelation always caused no end of trouble—scheming, fawning, backbiting.

So Sturbridge did recognize something of the hungry look she saw in the novice. What she did not know was what ill-considered maneuver had misfired, landing him with an escort duty that he so clearly considered to be some form of punishment.

"The Fatherhouse is beautiful," Sturbridge offered. "You are so fortunate to be able to live and work here."

He treated her to a withering look. One that said clearly, *You have no idea what you are talking about.* When he spoke, his voice had a bored, tour-guide quality to it.

"This building is one of the great treasures of the order. It was designed so that when Tremere—anywhere in the world—speak of the power and majesty of our house and clan, they have a worthy image to call to mind."

"It is breathtaking," Sturbridge said, ignoring the scornful look and choosing instead to focusing on his words. "How long have you studied here?"

He bristled a bit at the audacity of a personal question coming from one he so clearly considered *persona non grata*. In the end, the pleasure of talking about himself overcame his exaggerated sense of decorum. "I have been here, at the Fatherhouse, for over a score of years. Before that I was tutored privately in the house of my master and sire for a like amount of time, in order to prepare for my formal presentation to the court. It is shameful how some people dare drag themselves here without having acquired the barest rudiments of courtesy."

He did not turn to look at her as he spoke, so she smiled behind his back as she replied, "Courtesies bestowed lightly are esteemed lightly."

The phrase he had heard so many times from the mouth of Master Ynnis, his one-time tutor in the courtly arts, brought him up short. He gaped at her as she gracefully swept past him with the slightest inclination of her head. One of the very "lightly bestowed courtesies" she had mentioned. A gesture of mock deference.

If he had ever actually wondered what had become of his eccentric old tutor once Gerard himself had departed for court, it was only to conclude that pressing duties tutoring other exclusive clients surely kept the man occupied. But it was doubtful the novice ever gave his old instructor a passing thought. The maestro was an all-too-tangible reminder of a time when Gerard had been much more naive, uncertain of himself and the great destiny that lay before him.

He certainly would have been surprised to learn that, upon the occasion of her last visit to the Fatherhouse, a certain regent from the city of New York had been so taken with the unstudied grace and quirky wit of the man that she had immediately set about securing his transfer to the Chantry of Five Boroughs to serve as her master of novices.

Sturbridge got a half-dozen paces farther up the corridor before she heard the sound of him hurrying to catch up. The novice had considered the petty vengeance of leaving her to lose herself, but finally thought better of it. He had been entrusted with seeing her comfortably installed in the Vineyard Room. *As comfortably as possible,* he thought, wrinkling his nose at the thought of the disused accommodations. Although the commission was clearly beneath him, he intended to carry it out to the letter. Executing his duties precisely was another petty vengeance for him.

"They did not bother to tell me your name," he said, catching up to her. He sounded slightly out of breath; another affectation, she realized. If his earlier boasting were to be believed, he had been literally out of breath now for at least forty years. "An oversight, I'm sure." He arched his eyebrows slightly to make sure she knew that it had been no oversight, but rather an intentional slight. "Normally, I would not presume to burden you with personal questions...."

He means that normally, he could not care less, she thought. Sturbridge was not about to make things easier for him. She waited him out, forcing him to finish the thought, to struggle a bit.

"But you took a wrong turning just now," he said, "and when I went to call out to you, to bring this mistake to your attention, I realized that I did not know how to address you."

Sturbridge smiled. She thought that if she did give him her full name, or even just "Aisling," that it might be distinctive enough for him to piece things together with a little work. It was not a usual sort of name—not even among those as patently *unusual* as the undying magicians of House Tremere. "Medea" was a good name for a witch, she thought. Powerful, with an air of the classical about it, a sense of tradition. Or perhaps "Hildegarde," for the sensual, and devastatingly feminine, mystic. "Madame Blavatski" summoned up thoughts of spiritualist table-knockings married with ectoplasmic manifestations of the most discerning Victorian tastes.

What kind of name was "Aisling Sturbridge"? *A good Irish name,* she thought, hearing the words in her mother's thick lyrical sing-song. *Sturbridge. Bridge. Bride,* her mother's voice lilted on. *Never a bride. No, not our Aisling.*

"Bridgett," Sturbridge said, pushing the memory down and away. She thrust out a hand as if the gesture would complete the banishment, but she could still hear the laughing of her mother's voice. "And you were?" she challenged, a bit belligerently.

He ignored her outthrust hand and instead took her by the elbow and gently steered her back towards the proper course. "I am Gerard Egan," he said. "And here, at last, is your suite."

Gerard swept ahead of her, producing a key and holding it up for her inspection and admiration. He stooped over the ancient lock and struggled with it briefly. It squealed in protest, but eventually yielded to his prodding. He swung the door wide with a flourish, at the same time averting his face. "Your rooms, novitia."

The stale air displaced by the door's swing staggered out to meet them. It was hot, wet and stagnant like the breath of a drunk, and carried the sickly sweet reek of mildew. When Sturbridge made no move to precede him into the chamber, Gerard shrugged and entered.

"It wants for a bit of airing out," he called back over his shoulder. He delicately pressed one sleeve to his face and picked his way over to the room's single narrow window.

Sturbridge peeked hesitantly into the room. It was obviously no roughhewn cell, its floor lined with dirty straw. That had been her first fear. Realizing that there was nothing else for it, she straightened and swept boldly across the threshold.

Gerard was still struggling with the window, and Sturbridge feared his efforts might well shred the remains of the unraveling curtains. She guessed that they had been white in some earlier day, or perhaps a pale green. Now the drooping hangings were a dull tobacco-smoke brown. The tasseled tieback had long since been gnawed through by vermin and lay in a heap on the floor below. To the left of the window, the trailing drapes had nearly torn away entirely from their tarnished rod.

Judging from Gerard's grunting, the window may well have been painted shut in some decade past. The interior of the room certainly did not seem to have been disturbed for at least that long. There was a dull pop, and Gerard nearly thrust his hand through the grime-covered pane as the window surrendered and banged outward. Sturbridge could feel the air in the room stir slightly. The breeze forcing its way through the narrow aperture was a shade less hot. It brought with it the indignant buzzing of displaced insects and the thick smell of rotting vegetation. Still, it was a change from the mildew.

"There, that's better," Gerard said. "It's not much to look at, but..." He turned to face her and studied her for a moment appraisingly. Apparently, Sturbridge thought, he didn't consider *her* much to look at either.

"I don't suppose you're staying long," he said casually, feigning disinterest.

"I don't suppose so," she replied. "Still, we should do what we can with the place." She crossed to the inner door, fearing the worst. "Is it on the same key?"

"Ah, yes," he hurried forward, presenting the key before him with both hands as if it were a crown on a satin pillow. "The key to your palace, novitia. I trust that your visit here will be a pleasant one and that your business will be brought to a satisfactory conclusion. Now if there is nothing else..." He started for the corridor.

She laughed out loud. "Nothing else? You won't stay and brave the inner rooms then? I was under the impression that the novices here at the Fatherhouse would be made of sterner stuff."

He stiffened. "Of course," he replied curtly. He set his jaw, puffed out his chest and demanded, "Your key?"

She ignored his outthrust hand and inserted the large bronze key into the lock herself. Its handle was etched with a motif of vines and grapes. From the awkward angle of the key in the lock, she could tell already that the lock's inner mechanism was rusted shut.

She tried to turn the key once, just to maintain appearances, and then, setting her hand to the wood of the door itself, gave a gentle push. The door slid back noiselessly and effortlessly.

"I realize that this is all rather short notice," Sturbridge said, her voice arresting Gerard's progress back out the door, "but can you tell me when the cleaners might be through the rooms? That way I might arrange to stay out of their way until they have had a chance to go over the place. With any luck, I can find my way back to the rest of my party."

Gerard smiled. It was not a friendly sort of smile. "You can fetch water from the servants' quarters on the ground floor. I doubt you will be able to impress upon them the need to drop whatever they are doing to come and see to your needs, *novitia*. But you might beg of them some soap and a bucket and perhaps some rags."

Gerard was obviously still unaware of Sturbridge's actual station. Disabusing him of his mistaken impression might make things a bit easier, but she held back. Right now Gerard was her only point of contact among the Tremere of the Fatherhouse. If she were going to uncover what was truly going on around here, her discoveries would have to start with him. Lord help her.

Despite Gerard's looking down his nose at a "mere novice," it was plausible that he might let something useful slip in front of her, so long as he did not realize who she was. He was the type that would be boastful and lording around his subordinates, but guarded around his superiors.

"I'm sure I'll find my way. Thank you, Gerard."

For a moment, it seemed he might rebuke her for the familiarity, but he decided against it. Probably not worth his trouble to intimidate the newcomer. Given the fact that she didn't rate more comfortable accommodations, he doubted she would be staying with them for long. Probably just some messenger from a distant chantry. Still…

Gerard paused in the middle of bowing out. "What chantry did you say you were from?"

"Five Boroughs," Sturbridge said. "In New York."

He looked irritated. "I know where the Chantry of Five Boroughs is, novitia," he said scornfully. "I had classmate at one time who was transferred off to C5B. Not a very quick study, I'm afraid. Still, perhaps you know her…"

Sturbridge ignored the implied slight and shrugged apologetically. "I haven't been there long myself. But I do know most of the current novices. If she's still there, there's a good chance I might."

"I imagine she would still be there. It hasn't been that long and, as they say, there is only one way out of C5B…. Her name is Eva. Eva Fitzgerald. Do you know her?"

"I do," Sturbridge said. "She has done quite well for herself, a special favorite of the regent's. I had been unaware that she hailed from the Fatherhouse. No wonder the regent has taken to her."

"There was some kind of trouble, near the end," Gerard strained to recall the details. "Some embarrassment. I remember that I was not surprised when we were told that she would be leaving us. I am sure that C5B enjoys some measure of local respect. But I must confess, around here you have something of a sinister reputation, the lot of you. A transfer to your house is widely considered something of a cross between a suicide mission and a sentence to a girl's reform school."

Sturbridge smiled. "I guess that's not too far from the truth. C5B is a war chantry, Gerard. For the past ten years, we've been holding the front line in the war against the Sabbat. Mostly the 'volunteers' we get are the problem cases—the novices with either a colorful past, or a chip on their shoulders. Or something to prove."

"So, which are you?" he asked, trying to sound nonchalant.

Sturbridge shrugged. "A little of all three, I guess. Mostly, they nailed me on ambition." She leaned forward confidingly. "There are some, however, that would like to see this mission fail."

At this Gerard laughed out loud. "You will forgive me, novitia. I am sure you have already acquired many powerful and ruthless rivals. But you must admit that, unless you were forced to grow into your powers within these ancient halls—as I have—you have little room to boast of ambition and intrigues."

Sturbridge allowed him to wind himself down. "So Eva was ambitious even then? Before she came to us?"

"*Everyone* here is ambitious," he said. "To survive among wolves for even a week is an act of unbridled ambition. And often a foolish one." He gave her a meaningful look. "You will not be staying long?" It was not really a question.

Chapter Five
Silicon Homunculus

Helena pushed back from the keyboard and ground the heels of her palms into her aching eye sockets. She was stiff from her hours of devotion, crouched before the main interface of the chantry security-system daemon. This workstation was her altar. From here, she offered up binary prayers, trying fervently to reboot the system, to restore order to the delicate balance of electronic, mechanical and arcane wardings that comprised the backbone of the chantry's autonomic defenses. To breathe life back into her silicon homunculus.

Meandering trickles of blood and melted wax streaked the face of the monitor. The desk was ringed in black candles that gave off a stench of burnt fur. Each of the thirteen individual candle flames flickered on and off in time to the accessing of the hard drive.

Helena stretched and groaned. Even without glancing at the clock display in the lower right-hand corner of the screen, she knew that morning was creeping up on her. It was not the bone-weariness, nor the fuzzied thoughts—those were just symptomatic of the lack of sleep, the long hours. No, the sun always announced its presence to her with an unreasoning surge of panic, the feeling that she was running for her life, the certainty that she would be overtaken.

But not tonight. Helena keyed the final code sequence with a flourish worthy of a concert pianist. *Now, come on baby....*

"To grow a second tongue," came the lilting female voice, its singsong accent reminiscent of the west of Ireland. The security-system daemon. "As harsh a humiliation as twice to be born."

"At last! Thank God." Helena sighed with relief.

"Couldn't hurt," the daemon agreed.

Helena paid it no mind. "Run a full system diagnostic, please. I know for sure the local spirit guardians at the exeunt tertius and the novice *domicilium* are still off-line. See what you can do. I can step in to mediate if you run into trouble. Meanwhile, let me see if I can't start keying some of these interminable new security profiles and protocols from Vienna. Damned astors. With a little luck we'll be up and running again by sunrise."

"Entering diagnostic mode."

Two hours later, Helena snuffed out the last of the candles and swept up the remains of the protective chalk diagram. She logged out and cut the lights, but paused at the door, her hand still on the switch. "Good to have you back," she whispered to the empty room.

Head down, she trudged back towards her chamber. Her feet knew the way, though her mind was clearly elsewhere. The chantry corridors were, not surprisingly, nearly deserted at this hour. It was not until she reached the grand foyer that she caught sight of another person. She nearly bumped into him before she noticed him there. It was Himes. The astor's presence did little to improve her mood. He was probably the last person she wanted to see right now.

"Adepta," he said. "What an, erhm, pleasant surprise. I did not think to see you again tonight. We looked in on you earlier—that is to say, Mr. Stephens and I—but you seemed so intent upon your work that we did not want to disturb you. I take it you have had some success?"

Helena nodded. "It's done," she said, a touch of weariness peeking through her voice. "All of it. Or at least all I can do tonight. I rebooted the systems grid, got the security daemon back on line and input all your new profiles and protocols. I haven't had a chance to run any thorough testing on the changes yet, though, so you may still find a few bugs. Leave me a message and I'll sort out any problems tomorrow night. The novice *domicilium* is still offline. But that area should still be strictly off-limits anyway. After what happened there—"

She was about to say, "After what happened there last night," but then she realized that Himes was still unaware of the fiery rite that she had interrupted only the night before in the wreckage of the *domicilium*. And it was probably best that he remain unaware of it. She hurried on to cover up the uncomfortable pause. "I stationed a guard outside to keep folks the hell out of there."

Himes raised an eyebrow at her sudden and unexplained vehemence, but did not press her further on the subject. Instead he smiled and seemed genuinely pleased. "You have been busy. Excellent work, adepta." His voice was almost a purr of satisfaction; Helena's skin crawled. "And you have finished entering *all* the new security protocols that we entrusted you with?"

"All forty-six of them," she replied, without enthusiasm.

"Exceptional," Himes said. "Mr. Stephens will be—how do you say?—next to himself."

"*Beside* himself," she corrected gently.

"Ah, yes. Beside himself. And if I may interject something on a more personal note, I too am glad to see that you decided to make an appearance here. I know that it is late and you have already put in a long night's work. But it will mean so much to the other novices. To see that we are in accord on this matter."

He smiled and took her hand, pressing something large into her palm as he steered her into the grand foyer. She actually smiled as he turned her loose into the room, so relieved was she to be free of him. Patting her reassuringly on the shoulder, he padded his way back up the corridor towards the Hall of Daggers and Mirrors.

Helena watched the retreating figure until he vanished around a bend in the corridor. She was sure, right up to the last minute, that Himes would remember himself. That he would turn back and explain. But he left her staring, puzzled and exhausted, at the object he had pressed into her hand.

It was a stone.

Chapter Six
Suicide for Amateurs

*D*ead end.

Antigone didn't like the sound of that. All of her remaining leads pointed to Adam Graves, and now Graves was dead. Had he been overwhelmed with remorse at having set off the explosion at the Empire State Building and, in the process, killing all those bystanders? Or was it merely fear that the investigators—both mortal and supernal—were getting a bit too close?

She wondered if Graves had somehow gotten word of Jervais's death. If they had, in fact, been working together, it wouldn't be hard for Graves to have followed the trail of dead bodies to its logical conclusion: Whoever was on their trail would come after him next.

But things just didn't add up. The evidence here at the scene for one thing. A veteran of the deadly game of ledges since childhood, Antigone knew a little something about suicide. She had seen a number of attempts up close. And this place just didn't feel right to her.

A proper suicide attempt should be an elaborate production, with meticulous care given to setting, props and supporting cast. The latter should arrive at precisely the right moment to receive the full brunt of the emotional whammy, to repent for their mistreatment of the lead actor and, if at all possible, to witness the death-defying escape.

If Graves' death were a suicide, he was a rank amateur. There was no parting shot; that was what bugged her most. No note, no torn photographs, no bloody scrawl, no eleventh-hour phone call. The apartment hadn't been either tidied up or trashed outright. This wasn't the apartment of someone who was expecting to have complete strangers combing through his most personal possessions. A suicide has time to work these things out in advance. Time to brood, time to set his affairs in order. Graves' death lacked a certain *statement*. It seemed impulsive, random, meaningless.

Antigone's fingertips absently traced the pattern of bloodstains on the wallpaper, groping blindly for some pattern, some meaning that was eluding her. There was no doubt that Graves had met his end—and a violent one—here in this very room. But if it were not Graves who had planned this macabre performance, then who? Perhaps the supporting cast had shown up after all, but unexpectedly.

Antigone's thoughts chased themselves around in circles, but it was no good. If this were actually a murder, the identity of the gunman was a secret that Graves had taken with him into the silence of the tomb.

Antigone was startled from her musings by a tearing noise from the outer room. With a shiver she turned her back on the blood-speckled white porcelain—that pattern of blood-red streaks across a bone-white background reminded her of something, something recent and unsettling, but she couldn't quite put her finger on it. Silently, she slipped from the bathroom.

The lights in the living room blared to life, nearly blinding her. As she blinked her vision clear, she saw the outline of a hulking figure stooping through the tattered police tape. He was dressed in a bulky leather jacket shot through with shards of metal. The faded red Marlboro T-shirt looked a size too small for him. It didn't quite cover the gap between his navel and the top of the grubby oil-stained jeans. The mountainous man brushed aside the police tape that crisscrossed the doorway as if it were nothing more than a cobweb.

Antigone's gaze fell to the shotgun dangling from the end of his arm—an unspoken threat. She kept out of sight and studied him from just around the doorway to the dining room, waiting to see what his next move would be.

The newcomer's glance jerked nervously around the room, touching everything and settling on nothing. He saw the pattern in the dust of the desktop that said the computer was missing, but the big-screen TV was still there. That was wrong.

The police tape outside was wrong too. Not just a bad omen. Nobody left police tape up in nice corporate apartments like these. In the projects, maybe. But here, image was everything. The management company had to know that or they wouldn't have been doing business in this zip code for very long.

He almost turned around and walked back out. Still, there were none of the expected signals indicating a compromised rendezvous point—feathers just inside the threshold, the bones of small birds. Distractedly, he pushed the door shut for the second time, but it just bounced back at him again. He took in the splintered doorjamb and the fact that the deadbolt was still extended. *Kicked in*, he thought.

Everything about the place screamed trap. It was all a fabrication, a lie. It left a bad taste in his mouth. From the contrived series of (still-wet!) rings on the end table that were designed to lead him to think that two people had shared a bottle of wine here a few nights ago, to the figure furtively peeking around the doorway to the next room.

The stranger cleared his throat. "That wall's not so thick I can't shoot through it," he called, raising the shotgun to arm's length as if it were nothing more than a pistol.

Coming from anyone of less epic proportions, the threat would have been ludicrous. Nobody fired a shotgun unbraced and one-handed. The recoil from the blast would have spun him around like a leaf, if it didn't jerk the gun right out of his hand.

Antigone, however, wasn't sure she wanted to call him on it. She stepped out into plain sight and came slowly forward into the living room. "You ever knock, Charlie? You about scared the shit out of me."

Charlie lowered the shotgun. "Good, needed doing. Hell of a place for a get-together," he said. "Gotta hand it to you, Widow, you sure can pick 'em. Got anything in the fridge?"

He came forward, caught her forearm in his free hand and squeezed. Antigone gritted her teeth against the viselike grip and returned the greeting.

The moment stretched uncomfortably but still Charlie didn't release her. If anything he bore down harder. Antigone realized that, if there had ever been anything friendly in the gesture, it was there no longer. Still, she wasn't about to give him the satisfaction of giving in, of showing weakness. Antigone stared straight ahead at the white "l" in the Marlboro logo. Charlie towered over her; she barely came up to his chest.

He bent down slowly until they were face to face. His breath reeked of stale beer and cigarettes. "Felton says I can't trust you," he growled. "He says this is another set up."

"Then you've seen him." Antigone pounced on the revelation. She hadn't seen Felton since the night they confronted the Bonespeaker. "Is he all right? Where is he?"

Charlie shook his head, refusing to be turned aside from his point. "Yeh, I've seen him. He told me about your little showdown with the Bonespeaker. And about how you two had planned to kill him all along. He says you'll just try the same crap with me."

He clearly expected denials, explanations, protests of innocence. But what she said was, "Then why did you come?"

Charlie bore down harder, driving her towards her knees. "Because I trusted you. Hell, I was the one who brought Felton to you for help in the first place. And if you did double-cross my buddy, I'm going to kill you."

Antigone felt wrenching pain in her shoulder, knew she could not maintain her feet much longer under his steady, grinding onslaught.

"Felton," she said, "is full of shit." She stepped back suddenly, pulling the big man forward with her, unbalancing him. Charlie recognized the opening movements of the judo throw and quickly turned her loose—at the same time, breaking her own grip with a sharp downward twist.

She glided back gracefully, flowing away from him. The shotgun rose to fill the vacuum between them.

"It's not that easy," Charlie said. Antigone was not sure whether he was referring to her takedown attempt or to her dismissal of Felton's accusations. But she knew she had to say something, before the shotgun spoke up.

"But it's true. Look, Charlie, I'm not the one who set Felton up. I'm the one trying to get to the bottom of this. I saved his worthless butt, for Christsakes! Did he tell you that part?"

But Charlie was as tenacious as a mastiff. "You know what? I don't care anymore. I'm tired of this cloak-and-dagger shit. I'm tired of being in the middle of this thing between you and Felton. I think I'm going to break something, and you're at the top of the short list."

"You've got it all wrong, Charlie. Think for a minute. Have I ever lied to you before? Cheated you? Screwed you on a deal? We've been trading guns and bike parts for how long now? Two years, three?"

Charlie shook his head, but the shotgun never wavered. "Nope, you were always straight with me. That's the only reason you're still walking around now. But my guess is that that's all changed. This meeting tonight..." he gestured around him. "Jeez, look at this place! It's a fake, a setup."

"No, you're wrong, Charlie. This is about as real as it gets from here on in. Somebody died here. Last night, I think. Maybe the night before. But somebody else has gone to a lot of effort to obscure the signs. To make it look like a suicide."

"And to make it look like there's been a police investigation," Charlie snorted, "which is bullshit. But it still doesn't answer my main question. Why the hell should I care? So far as I'm concerned, you screwed my buddy and now I'm going to have to kill you. Nothing personal."

"Because the guy who lived here was Adam Graves. And the Bonespeaker told us—Felton and me—that Graves was the one who tipped him off about the bombing at the Empire State Building. Which means that Graves—"

"*Shit.*"

Charlie's head came around sharply, staring back over his shoulder towards the hall door at the sound of the invective. Taking advantage of the distraction, Antigone slipped inside the reach of the shotgun and wrapped one hand around the barrel, forcing it down and away. She needn't have bothered. The big man didn't resist her.

"I was hoping you might show up," Antigone said.

"Well, that's great," Felton replied from the doorway. "I suppose you'll be getting that ESP merit badge now."

"What the hell are you doing here?" Charlie demanded of the newcomer. "I thought we agreed that I would handle this and you would stay well the fuck away from here."

Felton shrugged and stepped forward into the room. He was dressed much as he was the last time she had seen him. Camouflage fatigue pants and an unadorned black T-shirt peeked out from under a long black felt coat that had seen better days. It occurred to her that Felton, a refugee from the prince, the chantry, the Conventicle, the FBI and the police, probably hadn't had a lot of opportunities to pick up a change of clothes. And anything that Charlie might loan him would easily swallow up two of Felton.

"And let you get yourself killed?" Felton demanded. "Not likely. You're all I've got left at this point, amigo. And I'll be damned if I'm going to let this witch take that away too."

"Come off it, Felton," Antigone said. "I'm not the one who landed you in this mess. Whatever's happened to you is your own damned fault and you know it. So how about we just cut the crap, okay?"

Felton rolled his eyes. "Fine by me. Less crap, more leaving. Come on Charlie, let's get out of here. You made the swap yet?"

Felton could see Charlie's hesitation. He hadn't been thinking about the handoff. Charlie muttered something and drew a folded and battered courier envelope from an inside pocket of his jacket. He tossed the bulging envelope on the floor between him and Antigone. It landed with a thump and slid a half-foot closer to her. "It's all there," he said. "You can count it if you want. Where's the hardware?"

Antigone made no move to retrieve the envelope.

"Yeh, Blackbird, tell him," Felton chimed in. "Where's the goods?"

Charlie blinked as if coming back to himself from a deep sleep. He seemed to realize for the first time that nowhere in the room could he see a box or crate or anything big enough to

contain the latest shipment of guns, explosives and bike parts—
Antigone's side of the bargain. The big man turned away from
her in disgust. "It's a set up. Let's get the hell out of here," he
said to Felton. He did not look up to see his partner's smirk.

"Charlie!" Felton punched him ungently in the shoulder.
"The money? Jeez, I don't know where your head is tonight."

"Leave it," Charlie said. "Let's just go."

Felton turned to Antigone. "You are a piece of work, you
know that? See you around, Blackbird. Wait up, Charlie."

He turned his back on her and started towards the door.
Something hit him in the back of the head and fell to the floor
with a metallic jangle.

He wheeled upon her. "You bitch. You damned—" Then his
eyes caught sight of the projectile lying at his feet. A metal ring
with a pair of keys, their chunky orange plastic grips printed
with bus locker numbers.

"You know your problem, Felton?" Antigone said. "You
don't know who your friends are. It's uncanny the way you
consistently turn on the only folks in the whole damned city
who are trying to help you. I take some consolation in the fact
that it's going to get you killed. And soon."

Felton scooped up the keys and brandished them at her like
a weapon. "With friends like you," he said, "who needs
enemas? You're a regular pain in the—"

Charlie's hand came down on his shoulder and shoved him
roughly back into the room. He closed the door behind them
and put his back against it. "So I was right about her, yes?"

As Felton seemed about to launch into another tirade,
Charlie shoved him towards the overstuffed sofa. Then he
folded his arms across his chest and leaned back against the
door in an attitude of impatience.

"Of course I was right," he said smugly. "And now you two
are going to settle this. I don't much care how you do it. You
can talk, you can shout, you can beat each other senseless, but

nobody's getting through this door until it's settled. That understood?" He gave the wooden door a series of reassuring pats that rattled it in its frame.

Chapter Seven
A Bedraggled Crown

"I like what you've done with the place," Dorfman said from the doorway. "It's kind of Early Industrial Coal-Cellar."

Sturbridge hadn't yet managed a sortie to try to win her way through to the servants' quarters for much needed mops, buckets and disinfectant. Thus far, she'd had to content herself with hauling the rotting drapes and bed linens to the fireplace, where she had a hearty blaze going. The fire flared and crackled with the death throes of entire colonies of moths and less-savory infestations.

"Come in," she said, "Just don't sit down on anything."

"I didn't catch you in the middle of something? I can come back later," Dorfman offered.

"Not a chance. I was just trying to decide about the mattress. Its condition is terminal, I'm afraid. I'm just wondering whether burning it might not do more harm than good."

"Hm, yes. The fumes. Quite possibly toxic. And certainly unpleasant and lingering in any event. Why are you doing this?"

"Well, if I'm actually to get any rest while we're here, I'll have to make the best of it. You don't know the way down to the servants' quarters? I need some supplies."

"I mean, why are *you* doing this? This place is unbearable. We're going back to Istavan right now. I'll drag him out of bed if I have to. You'll have accommodations suitable to your rank even if he has to—"

"I'm staying here."

"Well, then, he can at least get a cleaning crew up here. If they work around the clock, they might have this place habitable by next week."

"A little work isn't going to do me any harm," she said. "And it might take my mind off this meeting with Meerlinda."

"I told you, it's nothing to worry about."

"Nothing to worry about? Do you remember how you reacted when I told you about what had been going on? About the murders, about Eva, about the Children? You thought I was a raving lunatic."

"I never thought you were a lunatic."

"You didn't believe me. So you must have thought I was either a lunatic or a liar. I was giving you the benefit of the doubt."

"Look, you tell me that all of those murders at the chantry— those assassinations—that they were all engineered from the Fatherhouse in Vienna. How am I supposed to react? You have to admit that this is all a little... much."

"I realize that, Peter. But you've got to realize that there must be some powerful people behind this. We're taking a pretty big risk by coming here at all. I'm still not convinced that both of us won't be ash by morning."

"Aisling, you're being dramatic. Why should anyone here at the Fatherhouse want to see you destroyed? Or me, for that matter?"

"You still don't believe me," she accused. "Even after all you've seen back at the chantry. Even after everything I told you about Nina and—"

"We are not going to go into all that again. Look, I believe you. I believe that something has been done to you. Something involving Eva and the Children. But I don't understand any of this. So you've got to try to help me out here and the first step is to realize that I'm the one on your side, okay?"

Sturbridge shook her head. "I told you not to sit down on that."

Dorfman sprang back to his feet. Without thinking, he had settled down on the edge of an overstuffed armchair upholstered in an unsettling shade of green. A shade which, coincidentally, came away and stained the back of his slacks.

He swore. "I don't understand. Why would someone would go to all the trouble to arrange a string of murders at a chantry half a world away? It doesn't make any sense. What possible proof could you have to support these claims?"

"I've talked with the victims," she said flatly. "Not the murder victims, although they're all there too. But the victims of the grander plot—its pawns. Eva, Aaron, the ambassador, they are all within me now. Their secrets are my secrets."

"You want me to believe that you are somehow... cross-examining the dead?"

"Not the dead, exactly," she said. "More like the things that reproached the dead in their sleepless hours. Like your—"

"No," he said firmly. "Not like my anything. Look, I don't know what you did. How you found out about Nina. It was all very impressive, but for all I know it was just some improved mind-reading variation you've developed. I can't very well just tell Meerlinda that it's all been some big misunderstanding. No one's going to be satisfied with that, Aisling. No one."

"I'm not saying they'll be happy about it, Peter. I'm just telling you the truth. If you can't bring yourself to believe me, how are you going to keep them from dragging me before some formal tribunal? How are you—"

"Who is this 'them'? Be reasonable, Aisling. What choice do we have here?"

"So what's *your* plan?"

"It's simple. We see Meerlinda. We explain what's been going on back at Five Boroughs. We tell her that, between us, we've rooted out the responsible parties. And we tell her why it's never going to happen again. But if you go off on a tangent about some kind of sinister conspiracy..."

"How do you explain what's happened, then? Eva and the ambassador both came to Five Boroughs directly from the Fatherhouse. They manipulated and killed and tried to maneuver me into helping them release the Children. But something went wrong and now they are trapped within me. All of them. I have swallowed them utterly. And I don't know what it means or what I'm supposed to do about it."

"Who says you have to do anything about it?" Dorfman sighed and rubbed the bridge of his nose. "Look, Aisling, I know you've seen some things. Some very disturbing things. But even I'm having trouble buying into this stuff about your having 'eaten our dead.' And I tell you, Meerlinda is going to have an even harder time. She's not as predisposed to believe you as I am."

"I know that, Peter."

"So what exactly is it that you want me to do?"

"I just want you to believe me."

"I do believe you—"

"No, you don't. If you believed what I've been telling you, you'd be scared by now. Because there's something going on here. And you're caught up in it and know absolutely nothing about it. And that shortcoming, incidentally, is going to get us both killed."

"All right, I'm listening! How about you just tell me what exactly it is that we're supposedly going to burn for? Stumbling into the middle of some conspiracy? Because of some bad dreams? What?"

His tone was mocking, but his eyes bore into hers intently. Searching, compelling, trying to wrest from her her secrets. But she was prepared for him. In her eyes, he found only his own face, mirrored, inverted. He broke away and resumed a restless pacing.

"How am I supposed to help you if you won't even let me inside? I need the truth, Aisling. Hard facts and harder evidence."

She shook her head. "You're looking in the wrong place. I don't have the truth anymore. All that's left to me now are recriminations and failings, my own and those of others who are now lost to us."

"So what am I supposed to do? Tell Meerlinda that the ambassador's dead, case closed? You don't think she's going to want to know how he died? And why?"

"He died because he had become a liability. He was asking too many of the right questions. He was doing exactly what you're doing."

"Is that a threat?!"

"I'm not the one who killed the ambassador, Peter. But if I stood up before some formal tribunal and spoke the name of the one who did kill him... but I would not be allowed to go so far."

"Who killed the ambassador?" he asked in a more level tone of voice.

"She called herself Eva. Eva Fitzgerald. She was a novice under my care. I had come to look upon her as my protégée." Sturbridge laughed. It was a coarse, grating sound, like something tearing inside. "My most promising student, and no wonder."

"And you're telling me that she was some kind of plant, that she was sent from the Fatherhouse specifically to undermine you?"

"A plant? A curious little flower, certainly. One both beautiful and deadly. I am not certain that 'sent' is the right word. But she certainly came from here all the same."

A look of concern flitted across Dorfman's face. "Aisling, I..."

"The name she chose is suggestive, don't you think? I think she may have chosen 'Eva' because it was so close to that of my own dear daughter. Maeve. Certainly she chose her physical appearance for that reason, to play upon my sentiments—upon my loss, my regrets."

He put a hand upon her shoulder. "Aisling, enough. You need some rest. And you're not likely to get any here."

"But the 'Fitzgerald' is suggestive as well," Sturbridge pressed on unheeding. "Did you ever know any Fitzgeralds, I wonder, my little one? In London, perhaps. It is traditional there, I believe, for scions of the royal line to take that name. Or would that have been before your time?"

"Aisling!"

Her head came up sharply, but cocked to one side like that of a curious bird. She met his eyes. Within those depths, Dorfman saw, not the familiar mirrored surface of her carefully constructed defenses, but infinite depths of chill, murky waters.

There was a face there, a child's face, bobbing silently in time to some mysterious current. It was as radiant as a moon and framed in tangled strands of what must once have been golden hair. A bedraggled crown. But it was the eyes that drew his attention, would give him no peace. They were blue, a royal blue. But vacant, glazed over, lifeless.

Then, as Dorfman watched in growing horror, the face smiled up at him contentedly. The mocking bluish lips parted and contracted, mouthing silent words. Against his better judgment, Dorfman leaned in closer.

The thin whispered exhalation was stagnant and stank of a watery grave. He did his best to ignore the foul reek and bent even closer.

"Tell him," Eva whispered, exultant. "Tell Father that it is done."

Nothing more but a trickle of blackish waters passed her lips.

Dorfman wrenched away from her and found himself, once again, standing over Sturbridge, staring down at the trickle of blackish blood from her cracked lips.

Sturbridge's lips parted, but it was not her voice that came out. "Ask him if he's proud of me, Peter. Promise me that you'll ask him."

"Stop it!" He spun away from her and towards the door.

"Where are you going, Peter?" It was Sturbridge's voice this time, groggy, disoriented.

He turned back toward her for one more attempt. "Can't you see that this kind of thing isn't going to help us? You pull another stunt like that and Meerlinda's going to have you locked away somewhere. What we need are answers, not theatrics. Real answers. Now, I'm willing to admit that someone here at the Fatherhouse has been somewhat less than forthright about what happened at Five Boroughs—why Eva was there, why the ambassador was dispatched. And I don't like it when people keep things from me. Especially things that might get me staked for the dawn."

"But how will we even know the people we are looking for?" Sturbridge asked.

"We'll ask Meerlinda's help. And we'll keep a good eye out for anyone who is trying to kill us. Don't worry, I am quite accomplished at finding people who are trying to kill me. In the meantime you will remain here. And by 'here' I mean in your quarters. I will put you officially under house arrest if I have to."

He was prepared for an argument on this point. When she made no protest, he regarded her with open suspicion.

"I mean it. Don't fight me on this, Aisling. I've got to know that you're going to be safe until I can return. I'm going for Istavan. I'll be back as soon as I can. In the meanwhile, you're confined to quarters. Doctor's orders. And I want you to stay the hell away from everybody."

"All right," she said. "But I'm coming with you to see Meerlinda."

"Tomorrow," he said. He paused halfway out the door. "And keep the door locked. I'll come for you first thing tomorrow night. I promise."

"It's a date," she said.

Chapter Eight
An Old Friend

"I don't believe this," Felton said throwing up his hands in disgust. "I've got nothing more to say to her. Let's get out of here."

He tried to push past Charlie, but the bigger man cut him off, planting one hand firmly in the center of his chest. "Nope. Nobody's going anywhere until this is settled."

Felton swore and rounded on Antigone. Despite his protest that he had nothing more to say to her, he was obviously struggling with a long list of grievances that were bubbling towards the surface.

"Oh, let's just get this over with," Antigone interrupted, giving him a shove that sent him backpedaling towards the door once more. She took up a fighting stance. "Go ahead, take your best shot."

"Christ," Felton muttered, regaining his balance and looking back and forth between Charlie and Antigone. "Hung out to dry between a pair of idiots."

Charlie snorted and Felton wheeled upon him. "What are you laughing at?" he demanded.

"Nothing," Charlie said, still chortling. Then, when Felton did not relent, Charlie admitted sheepishly, "You said, 'Christ hung up between a pair of idiots.' You know, Christ? Hung up between a pair of—"

"Shut up, Charlie, all right?" He turned back to Antigone. "So that's it? That's how you want to do this? I just haul off and flatten you and we can all get out of here and never have to look at each other again? I think I can handle that."

"Waiting," Antigone snapped.

Felton walked straight up to her, balling his right hand into a fist. Antigone made no move to block the blow or sidestep it as Felton hauled back. He socked her in lightly in the shoulder.

"Tag, you're it. And we're out of here. Come on, Charlie. It's been a kick," he called back over his shoulder. "We'll have to do this again real soon."

Her kick caught him in the back of the knee and it buckled. As he staggered and turned, her arm shot out, the heel of her palm catching him beneath the chin and snapping his head back. He fell heavily against Charlie.

"Son of a bitch." Felton's hand came up to his mouth and came away red from where he had bitten his lip. Charlie gave him a shove with the flat of the shotgun, sending him lurching back out into the room.

"Normally, it's against my principles to hit a lady. Aw, who am I kidding?" He took a roundhouse swing, but Antigone glided back out of its path. It was more a feint than a real threat. The follow-up strike, however, was something else altogether — hard, straight and lightning fast. She caught it with the back of her forearm, narrowly knocking it aside.

It was only then she realized that his hand was not empty, but clenched around a sharpened wooden stake. That was a bad sign. It was ominous enough that Felton was looking for a far more permanent solution in this conflict than she was. But it was far worse that she hadn't even seen him pull the weapon.

She didn't have a lot of time to reflect, though, as his attacks renewed with ferocity and blazing speed. Antigone could no longer keep track of the individual blows. Her body was running on pure instinct now. At one point, Antigone managed to gain a moment's breathing space by catching him in an aikido maneuver that Helena had taught her, sending Felton crashing into the end table. Both collapsed to the floor in a tangle.

Antigone took advantage of the brief pause to make sure that Charlie had not repented of his earlier resolution to stay out of this. The burly biker had come forward a few steps, craning to follow the action, but the shotgun still hung limp at his side. There was a slight rustle of worried whispers from the hall outside.

Then Felton was up again, hurtling towards her, and such concerns vanished beneath the flurry of blows. If the sounds of their struggle did attract unwanted company, Charlie would just have to deal with it.

The stake was darting in and out so fast now that it seemed to leave motion trails in its wake. Antigone's hands and forearms were numb from the stinging rain of blows and blocks. Her ears rang with the slap of flesh on flesh. And everything around her seemed to slow down.

Antigone didn't know how much longer she could keep this up. She knew that, despite her security training, Felton was by far the cannier and more experienced fighter. He had tempered his fighting edge with more than a decade of nightly combat in the streets against the worst the Sabbat could muster. Against that, Antigone's usual sparring partners, the novices at the Tremere chantry, were sadly undermatched.

She needed to try a different approach, and quickly.

Concentrating all her attentions on the dance of the deadly stake, she allowed his off-hand punch to snake through her guard. It landed squarely on her jaw with more force than she would have thought an opponent of his size—or any size much less than Charlie's mountainous bulk—could have mustered. Her sight glazed over with red and she blinked rapidly to clear it. It was a moment before she realized that the reason that everything around her was refusing to focus was that she was falling backward. She crashed into the wall, trying to roll with the impact. The sharp cry of protest from her shoulder told her that it had borne the brunt of the impact, and none too stoically.

She straightened, clearly favoring her left side and the injured shoulder. "Had enough yet?"

If she had hoped to goad him into some desperate attack, she was disappointed. Felton stalked closer with all the patience of a big cat. Closing in for the kill. From this distance, she could see the jagged tips of his fangs peeking past his split lip.

She pushed off the wall and did her best to stand tall before him. There was resignation in her eyes. Her hands, balled into tight fists in anticipation of the blow that was already descending upon her, stayed down flat against her sides.

Felton's fist reared high, drawing back over his shoulder. It drew her gaze back with it, focused on the point of the stake hanging over her like a judgment. She made no move to dodge or block the blow.

Then, with all the weight of his body behind it, it smashed down upon her.

Chapter Nine
The First Stone

Helena gazed dumbly at the object in her hand. A rock. Then she walked out into the grand foyer and the significance of the object broke through the fog of exhaustion. In the very center of the high vaulted room, chained between two pillars, stood a novice. She was clearly in the clutches of the Beast. Her eyes filmed over with blood rage, she strained against her bonds and lashed out at any who dared approach her. She was ringed by a circle of her peers, all gazing on in mingled horror and fascination. Those who dared to even meet the ravaging madness in the girl's eyes turned away again quickly. The imprisoned novice snarled and bared her fangs at any hint of movement around the circle, twisting and writhing painfully in her chains.

As Helena drew closer, she could see that the novice was bleeding freely from several wound about her head and face. With growing alarm, Helena recognized a hint of the familiar visage obscured behind a mask of hurt and bestial rage. It was Anise! It couldn't have been two hours before that Helena had relieved the youngest member of her security team and sent her back to the novice *domicilium* for the night. But why then was she here? And like this?

"What the hell is going on here?" Helena snarled, startling the ring of novices like a murder of frightened crows caught in the act of pillaging. Several of them exchanged inarticulate and worried expressions.

"I said, what the *hell* is going on around here?!" Helena raged, advancing upon them. Only then did she realize that her fist was still clutched around the object that Himes had pressed into her hand. The stone.

Another novice in the ring guiltily tried to conceal her own stone within the sleeves of her robes. Helena glared at her and pounced. "You," Helena addressed her directly. "Speak up!"

"I... I'm sorry, adepta. I couldn't... I mean, I just couldn't. Even like this, it's still Anise. She is... She sleeps in the bed next to mine," she finished awkwardly, as if that explained everything.

Helena seemed about to explode. "What the hell do you mean..." she began.

The novice let out a squeak and, turning her head aside, hurled the stone at Anise. It was a clumsy shot and hit the maddened creature in the shoulder. "There!" she blurted, not meeting the eyes of anyone. "I've done it, damn you. Damn you all! Now get away from me. Just leave me alone!" She broke from the circle and streaked off towards the novice *domicilium* in a flutter of skirts.

Helena stared after her openmouthed. A few of the other novices took this opportunity to edge away quietly toward the other exits from the chamber.

"Nobody leaves this hall," Helena hissed, "Until..."

Her words prompted another half-hearted volley of stones. Anise howled in pain and frustration.

"Stop it!" Helena shouted. "That's not what I meant! Stop it right now." The situation was getting rapidly out of hand. "Security system, please incapacitate the next person who tries to cast a stone."

"Checking clearance," the daemon replied amicably. "Helena, Adepta. Insufficient access. Sentence of death by stoning ordered by Stephens, Astor. To override, please summon Stephens, Astor, or Dorfman, Peter, Lord Inquisitor."

"Emergency override," Helena snarled through clenched teeth. The other novices made no further attempt at stealth and broke for the nearest exits. "Override code: *Gallia est omnis divisa in partes tres*."

"Override code overwritten and disabled," replied the lilting sing-song. "Further attempts to interfere with prescribed sentence will result in the summoning of an emergency response team."

"An emergency response team," Helena sputtered, hardly able to speak past her rising ire. "I *built* the damned emergency response teams. I *trained* the emergency response teams. I…"

Suddenly realizing that she was alone in the room aside from the still struggling Anise, Helena broke off cursing. This was pointless. Anise was *on* the damned emergency response team. *No, let it go.*

There was no point in arguing with the system-security daemon. She knew some of the new programming might be buggy. She hadn't had a chance to test it all thoroughly yet. If anything, it was her own fault and standing here arguing with the damned machine was not exactly going to inspire confidence in any of the novices who had hung back just outside the chamber to see how this colorful confrontation would play itself out.

There would be plenty of opportunity to reprogram the system. Tomorrow.

She looked over at Anise and the novice growled at her, regarding her warily. "Okay, maybe tonight," she said aloud. "I'll get you out of here, don't worry about it. I've just gotta have a little talk with Stephens. And then reprogram the system. An hour, tops. I promise."

Unfortunately, there wasn't much more she could do for the girl right now. Her first instinct was to brave the fangs and claws, to just walk right up and snap the chains. Helena was quite certain, however, that such an act would only prompt the security daemon to a more determined intervention. And Helena was all too familiar with the deadly array of firepower the daemon could bring to bear if pressed.

She hoped at least her tone of reassurance would penetrate through to Anise. It was all she had to offer at the moment. As Helena stormed from the room, she caught sight of the last few novices who still hung back, peering in from just outside the room. She called out, "Security system, please implement curfew procedures. All novices to be returned to *domicilium* immediately and to remain there until sunrise. Acknowledge."

If she couldn't get Anise away from here, Helena could at least ensure that she would not be intruded upon further in her pain and humiliation.

"Checking clearance… Confirmed," the daemon replied pleasantly. Then its voice came at Helena from all directions at once, issuing from not only the room's com ports, but also those in all the surrounding corridors. "Curfew protocol now in effect. All novices have exactly five minutes to report to the novice *domicilium*. Doors will seal in five minutes and not reopen until sunrise. Repeat: Curfew protocol now in effect…"

Without a passing look back at Anise, Helena struck out for the Hall of Audiences to find Stephens.

Chapter Ten
Three Feet Tall in Wet Sneakers

The first thing that Antigone realized when she came to was that her skull was on fire. *No,* she thought upon further investigation, *that isn't precisely true. It just feels like my skull is on fire.*

She groaned and one hand fluttered to her face, but it was sharply batted away. Her entire arm flopped back to the hardwood floor. "Quit fooling around or it's not going to set right." It was Felton's voice.

Antigone's eyes fluttered open onto darkness. "What's not going to what?" she said, but all she got for her trouble was an inarticulate mumble and a renewed flash of fiery pain in her head. It sounded like she was trying to talk around a mouthful of food, which was something she had not in fact done since her unfortunate (if brief) stay at Miss Jane Simpson's Academie for Girls back in Scoville. And that had been over eighty years ago.

"How many fingers?" Felton was asking. He shoved something right up into her face, but she couldn't quite manage to make contact with it to push it away.

"How many?" he repeated. "Charlie, get us a little light in here for Christsakes."

A painful brightness swam closer and she tried to turn away, only to find that her head was sandwiched between two sofa cushions, which had apparently been arranged to keep her from doing precisely that.

"Talk to me, Blackbird," Felton coaxed. "How many?" He kept waving something in her face and it was a moment before she realized it was his hand. Then the silhouette swam into focus.

"Very funny, asshole," she said, knocking his hand with its single extended digit away. She tried to sit up and failed, but a hand caught her from behind before she could smash back down to the floor again.

"She sounds fine," Charlie offered.

Antigone tried again, this time with more success. "What the hell happened? Oh." Her memory of the fight came flooding back to her. Her head was still foggy and her jaw blazed from where Felton had brought his fist, stake and all, crashing down upon it.

Her hand went again to her face, more carefully this time. Felton had done a good job of resetting the dislocated jaw. She imagined he had more than a bit of experience in quick patch-ups on the fly. She willed the flow of healing blood to the area to help complete the job.

"You feel better now?" Antigone asked through clenched teeth.

Felton considered. "Some," he said. "You?"

"Much better, thanks," she lied. "Now do you think we can get back to business?"

"I guess so. No hard feelings?" He stuck out a hand.

She took it and let him haul her to her feet.

"Aw. And me without my Polaroid," Charlie muttered. He looked very pleased with himself.

"Shut up, Charlie," Felton snapped at him without turning from Antigone. "So how 'bout you explain why you set up this whole thing with Charlie and me here tonight. I'm guessing it's more than you just wanted to get your clock cleaned."

Antigone let the taunt wash over her. "Come and see," she said. She staggered a few paces towards the darkened back rooms of the apartment before she got her legs under her. Charlie threw Felton a questioning glance, but the latter shrugged and followed her.

In the tiny bathroom, Antigone flicked on the light switch. Felton's pace slowed and he whistled low, struck for the first time not only by the sight but also by the scent of the carnage. Someone had done a quick and sloppy job of scrubbing splattered blood and gore from the wallpaper. Felton could see the main concentration of the stains was high on the wall above the toilet, the wall opposite the mirror. To his mind, that spoke of someone standing over the sink—staring fixedly into the mirror at the butt end of the pistol jutting from his mouth.

Antigone retrieved her overstuffed bag from the vanity, where she had left it earlier when Charlie burst into the apartment. "We need to find out who killed Graves—"

"Um, no offense, Blackbird," Felton interrupted. "But it looks like Graves took matters into his own hands here."

"We don't know that," Charlie said. "Somebody else might have forced him in here at gun point and blown his brains out for him."

"Sure, that *could* have happened," Felton said. "If the gunman was about three feet tall and standing in the sink at the time. Look at the damn splatter marks."

Charlie scowled. "They could have been wrestling for the gun, like this." He pressed through the doorway to demonstrate. Squeezing in front of the mirror, he grabbed Felton's wrist and sank to one knee as if struggling for control of a pistol.

"This is stupid," Felton said breaking away and retreating from the claustrophobic room to a position just outside the doorway. "As much as I'd love to spend my entire evening throwing each other around some dead guy's apartment," he said, "this still isn't going to tell us squat about how he died or why. So the guy decides to redecorate the inside of his bathroom with the inside of his skull. So what?"

"But if it was someone else who pulled the trigger," Charlie continued stubbornly, "we need to know who. Graves knew the Empire State Building was going to blow. And he knew when. Either he set that bomb himself, or someone in the know tipped him off."

"So how's standing around here going to tell us that?" Felton challenged. "If anyone actually witnessed Graves' death, now that might be something to go on. But my guess is that, if anyone else was here when Graves got shot, he's not talking either."

"Because he'd be the killer," Charlie insisted.

Felton let out an exasperated sigh. "So all we've got to do is comb the entire city for someone three feet tall, with an unregistered handgun and wet sneakers from standing in the sink...."

"Unless there was another witness," Antigone said.

"Oh sure," Felton said. "Maybe the circus was in town and a whole parade of sideshow freaks came along to enact their vengeance on the successful Internet company PR exec!"

"A witness who is still here," Antigone said, in an ominous tone, "in the apartment."

This pronouncement brought Felton up cold. He was acutely aware that, standing framed in the light of the bathroom doorway, his back was exposed to the rest of the dark and silent apartment. Very slowly, he turned around and put his back to the wall, scanning the darkened dining room.

Charlie cursed.

"What's wrong?" Felton hissed, "You see something?"

"The shotgun," Charlie whispered. "Left it in the—"

It was Felton's turn to curse as he gestured his friend to silence.

"I think," Antigone said, suppressing a smile, "that you misunderstand me. There is no one else here in the apartment with us."

"Then what the hell are you talking about?" Felton demanded.

"I will show you," she said, and began unpacking the contents of her bag onto the vanity. Candles, chalk, a handful of black feathers. An oversized straight razor, a velvet bag whose contents rattled like old knucklebones. The skeleton of a bird bound in copper wire. And two halves of a blood-streaked bone-white mask.

"I think it is time, gentlemen," she said, "that we reconvened the Conventicle."

"Oh no it's not!" Felton objected. "The last time we went back there, we both very nearly ended up dead. Or maybe you don't remember that?"

"We're not going anywhere, Mr. Felton," Antigone said, raising the two halves of the mask to her face. With a sickening squelch, the broken pieces clung to her face, sealed in place by the thin layer of blood lining the inside of the mask—the Bonespeaker's congealed vitae. "We're going to reconvene the Conventicle right here."

Felton stared at her a moment in disbelief. The stark avian mask met his gaze and returned it levelly. He had glimpsed the features of that mask many times before in darkened meeting spaces. Now, however, it had a very different aspect. The chalky white mask looked almost theatrical in the bright light, its daubed white paint swirled and patchy in places. But what held his attention were the angry red streaks, the trails of blood running in parallel—but counterintuitively, *upwards*—from the mask's base to its crown. The Bonespeaker's blood had spilled as he hung suspended and inverted, swinging like a macabre pendulum, from the theater loft.

Felton glanced back and forth nervously between that visage and the front door, checking the path to freedom and safety. "I knew this was a set up!" He turned angrily upon Charlie. "I told you this was a set up. We're getting out of here, right now. Before anyone else shows up."

The big man didn't budge. Antigone turned back to her preparations.

"I said, we're getting out of here," Felton insisted.

"You just don't get it, do you?" Charlie replied.

"Get what? There's nothing to get. We've talked about this before. We can't trust the other members of the Conventicle. You know that. You think they're all going to thank us for offing the Bonespeaker? Maybe throw us a little party? Of course not! They're going to be pissed. Probably pissed enough to try to kill us."

Charlie tried to interrupt but Felton shouted him down. "No, I take that back. They're not *all* going to be pissed. A few of them were probably just infiltrating the Conventicle on the orders of the prince. Those guys probably don't give a shit that the Bonespeaker finally got what he deserved. But the prince's men have reasons of their own for wanting us dead, don't they? Am I missing anybody here?"

"Yup," Charlie said, folding his arms across his chest and leaning back against the wall with a self-satisfied grin.

His agreement checked Felton's tirade. "Please," he said, "do elaborate. I know this is a bad idea already, but feel free to go ahead and pile on even more evidence to support my case."

"Us," Charlie said. "The three of us. We *are* the Conventicle now. Those other guys, well I can't say that they'll ever figure out for sure what happened. Some of them would have just drifted away after the bombing anyway, decided to lay low for a while until it all blew over. Most of them are probably still in hiding. Those with balls enough to answer the Bonespeaker's summons — on that night when you two busted in there — they would have showed up to find the signs you left that the meeting site was compromised. The body of a bird on the steps. They would have turned right around and gone home again to await the next call. A summons that's never going to come now."

"And that leaves us," Antigone said. "Can you hit the lights, please?"

Both men turned at the sound of her voice. The vanity was now covered with a layer of ground chalk. Pressed down into the powdery layer were three unlit candles, forming a ring around the sink. One white, one red, one black. The chrome stud behind the faucet had been pulled up, stoppering the sink. The basin was filled to a knuckle's depth with freshly fallen vitae, and a raw pink puckered wound peeked from Antigone's sleeve.

"Shall we begin?" she asked.

Chapter Eleven
Gas Lamps and Gilt Cherubs

Dorfman was as good as his word. Sturbridge didn't know what he had said to the castellan, Istavan, but not a half hour after Dorfman left her, a small army of cleaners and porters had shown up at her door.

He kept his other promise as well, but Sturbridge had been up for an hour already when his knock came on the door of the Vineyard Suite. Her rest had been troubled by visions of a bubbling dark tarn and veined bluish flesh clamoring from its depths. She awoke with recriminations ringing in her ears—accusations of wrongs committed hundreds of years before by people Sturbridge would never know.

Dorfman ushered her from the squalid rooms and led her through an opulent labyrinth—a maze of balustraded galleries overlooking a moonlit garden, a conservatoire, a tiled courtyard, further interlocking galleries—until she felt quite lost. Each corridor contained eyes that studied them circumspectly from behind a veneer of bored disinterest, and voices that whispered and tittered at their passing. If anyone felt the urge to approach the two visitors, however, Dorfman's pace and glowering demeanor discouraged them.

"Where are we going?" Sturbridge said at last. She did her best to remain composed, but the strain of another evening of unwelcome scrutiny and casual judgments was already starting to wear upon her.

"Meerlinda's apartments," Dorfman said. "She's the one who got me into this fool assignment. She can damned well be the one that finds some way to get us all back out of it."

His sudden vehemence surprised her. "Not that you're bitter. But what does Meerlinda have to do with all this?"

He reluctantly slowed his pace to match hers, but his body seethed with nervous energy seeking outlet. "Too much, I'm afraid," he said. "It's all dominoes. Look, when the situation back home in D.C. became untenable, Meerlinda was the one who suggested that it might be 'best for all concerned' if I returned here to the Fatherhouse for a while. She's my boss, so she calls the shots. I am accountable to her; you're accountable to me. And Meerlinda's responsible only to her peers on the Council of Seven. That's how the hatchet falls."

"I understand all that," Sturbridge said. "What I don't get is—"

"If we can just convince Meerlinda, everything is fine. I'm off the hook, you don't get dragged before some tribunal, and maybe we can figure out what the hell is going on with you and these… visions. All right?"

"What choice do we have?" Sturbridge asked.

"That's the spirit."

She felt as if they had been wandering the marbled corridors for hours when at last Dorfman paused before a daunting iron-bound portal. The weathered oak looked sadly out of place among the baroque splendor of the surrounding galleries. It should have barred the way to some dungeon cell, rather than languishing here amidst the lavishness of the vaulted ceilings, gilt scrollwork and airy colonnades.

The door was unadorned save for a blackened iron grillwork that formed an arch-shaped window in the door's uppermost reaches. The grill must have been intended for ventilation. Its slats were too tightly spaced and high-set to allow anyone to really see through it. No hint of light emanated from within the chamber.

"Here we are," Dorfman said.

Sturbridge, wary of treachery, did not like the look of this place. "Wait a minute," she said, grabbing Dorfman's arm to get his attention. "We had a deal, remember? I said I'd come back to Vienna with you, but on my own terms. Not as a prisoner."

"Relax," he said. "These aren't your new apartments, they're Meerlinda's."

"Meerlinda's?" Sturbridge repeated. She had never met the councilor face-to-face. On Sturbridge's previous visit to the Fatherhouse, they had been in the midst of a delicate situation. No one had even suggested that she be given the grand tour. Sturbridge wondered what kind of person willingly surrounded herself with such crude trapping in the midst of all the finery of the Fatherhouse. All of which was surely hers for the asking.

"Disappointed?" Dorfman asked.

"No, it's just..."

"An eyesore?" He chuckled. "Istavan, the castellan, has been trying to impress upon her the need to update the decor for years. At this point, I think he'd settle for anything within the last four centuries. But I believe that he has begun to despair of even that effort."

Sturbridge ran a hand along the rough grain of the door's surface. "No," she said firmly. "I like it. It has a solidity about it. A weight of history."

Dorfman gave her a curious look. "Look around you," he said. "This is an actual seventeenth-century palace. This is not some colonial restoration. You really think this place needs some worm-eaten old door to give it a sense of history?"

Sturbridge patted the door reassuringly. "I'd think it would be very grounding for her. To have something of your own youth around you. Imagine always feeling hundreds of years out-of-date—even among the trappings of the seventeenth century! No, I think I should like something of my own mortal years to comfort me when I grow old and weary of the world and of things that change. I shall surround myself with gas lamps and gilt cherubs. With—"

"They have a very strict policy against gas lamps here," Dorfman assured her. He rapped a quick staccato on the door. No answer.

"Nobody home. Now what?" Sturbridge asked.

Dorfman cursed. He grabbed the iron ring that served as a doorpull and rattled it, to no noticeable effect. When he bent over the lock, Sturbridge glanced about them apprehensively.

"What exactly are you doing?" Sturbridge asked in a hushed voice. Even here, she felt the weight of eyes upon them. Her apprehension was not allayed by Dorfman's furtive manner as he bent over the lock.

Craning forward to peek over Dorfman's shoulder, Sturbridge could see that the keyhole was ringed with the same blackened iron that bound the door. The keyhole itself was oversized, so much so that it appeared almost a decorative conceit. Dorfman ran his fingertips over the rough-hammered surface.

"We wait," Dorfman said in a low voice, fumbling with the lock. Nothing about his manner, however, suggested patience. He was clearly rattled. He had been dreading this interview; that much was plain from the way his pace had dragged the closer they got to this daunting portal. He had had too much time to construct the scene in his mind, to rehearse his explanations, his excuses, his conciliatory offers. Meerlinda's absence swept all that away. It shook him, threw him off his game.

Sturbridge felt a moment of apprehension when she realized what he was doing. Was Dorfman really going to pick the lock to the councilor's private study? "Peter, do you think this such a good idea…?"

She saw that he had managed to lodge the tip of his index finger within the keyhole. Somehow she took little reassurance in the fact that lockpicking was obviously not a vice he engaged in with any regularity. In fact, looking at him standing there—bent double, cursing, one finger stuck in the keyhole—she realized that she might be hard pressed to come up with a worse practitioner of that ancient art.

"Here, let me," she offered, trying to push past him. There was a sharp *snick* from the keyhole. Then it suddenly surrendered Dorfman's finger, which came away with a bead of crimson spreading across its tip.

He cursed and stuck it in his mouth, sucking on it. He muttered something that might have been, "Hate that part."

Then, to Sturbridge's astonishment, the door swung inward.

She shook her head. "I'm afraid that effort's not going to win any points for technique," she said.

"Okay, wise guy. Next time, you can go first. Of course, the next lock might be a lot bigger, say the size of a guillotine."

"You know lockpicking is not traditionally done with the bare hands right? I mean, they have tools for this sort of thing."

"Lockpicking? Oh, I see. No, I wasn't picking the lock, I was letting it identify me. It only opens to those whose blood it recognizes, I'm afraid. Of course, it will bite just about anybody. After you."

He gestured into the darkened interior of the room. There was a flickering light set upon a desk across the room, about as bright as a candle flame. Hesitantly, Sturbridge entered the councilor's private chambers.

Chapter Twelve
Brutal, Squalid and Terrifying

Felton started to object, but Charlie elbowed him sharply in the ribs. "Don't say anything stupid, okay? Don't you get it? It's just the three of us now. We're all we've got left. I guess it's actually been that way for a while now, only some of us were too stubborn to admit it."

Felton still wasn't convinced and there was a note of anger or bitterness in his voice. "It's not that easy."

"Sure it is, buddy. Nothing easier. In fact, I wonder if this isn't how it all started—the Conventicle, I mean. Back in the day, at the height of the Sabbat occupation. Just a handful of folks stranded behind enemy lines with nothing left they could count on."

Felton hadn't thought much about the origins of their circle of conspirators before, and he wasn't in any kind of mood to start now. He just assumed that the Conventicle had always been around—just like the Sabbat—and always would be, if only folks like he and Charlie kept up the good fight each night.

Only now there was no more Sabbat. There was no more good fight. There wasn't even any Conventicle. Just three sorry has-beens clinging to some over-romanticized image of the past. A past that was—if he was honest with himself—nothing to get nostalgic about. Brutal, squalid and terrifying.

Look at us! he thought. Going through the motions of some sad pantomime that had played itself out ages ago. Repeating the same incomprehensible invocations that had been handed down to them—but without meaning or conviction. The familiar gestures no longer brought a sense of well-being, of being grounded within tradition.

Felton found himself wondering (damn Charlie!) about that first gathering of the Conventicle, when the original band of conspirators had come together to pledge themselves. But to what? They'd promised to bind their fates together, to forge a chain stronger than the sum of its individual links. But was there nothing more to it than that—just the old "safety in numbers"?

Somewhere along the line, they had lost even that tempering fire. The members of the Conventicle still went through the motions, but it was different now. They had become little better than automata, wind-up toy soldiers, painted in the bright colors of mystical mumbo-jumbo.

Felton had killed, time and again—even been willing to die—to carry out the will of the Conventicle. That unquestionable justice of the collective. And, with a twinge of loneliness, nostalgia and even a touch of self-loathing, he realized he missed it. Missed it terribly.

It was the sense of belonging, more than anything else. The sense of being exactly in the place that had been prepared for him, ordained by God or fate or chance or whatever. Everything that had gone before—all the choices and sacrifices, all the victories and failures—they all led to that one place.

It was more than where he belonged. It was somewhere that needed him as well. He was respected for his skill, his determination. The Conventicle might be a bizarre, insular and ultimately deadly community. But it was a community that he was an integral part of. It was not only somewhere he belonged, it was somewhere that belonged to him. And in these nights of ever-increasing personal isolation—masquerading as a time of global community—that belonging mattered.

And here we are again, he thought. *About to start the madness all over again. To invoke the Conventicle. We are those who, having failed to learn from the mistakes of our own personal history, are doomed to repeat it. Night after night. Rising, hunting, killing, feeding. Nothing more than ambulatory corpses without the good sense to lie down and be still.*

"What the hell do you folks want from me?" he demanded aloud. Already he could feel some essential part of him slipping away, being subsumed into the need of the group.

"A light, for starters. If you've got one," Antigone said gently. She held out a long, tapering candle towards him expectantly.

Felton fished around in an inside coat pocket and found a chrome Zippo. He laid it down on the vanity, but kept his hand pressed on top of it.

"I'm not sure I want to bring the Conventicle back," Felton said. "Maybe it's better that all this ends now. That we just forget about it, let it lie down and be dead."

"Who are you, stranger, and what have you done with my poor idiot buddy Felton?" Charlie demanded. "I can't believe I just heard those words coming out of your mouth. Aren't you the same guy who was moping around my apartment just a few weeks ago, moaning about how you couldn't just let it all go?"

"Yeh, well, maybe I can now, all right?" Felton said. "Maybe it's time we all just let it all go."

"Bull," Charlie said. "You can't walk away. You're being given a chance to have it all back, Felton. Just like it used to be. Only this time, you'll be in on the ground floor. Instead of getting shot at, you'll be calling the shots. It's what you always wanted."

"Yeh, well, maybe I don't want it anymore."

"What do you want, Mr. Felton?" Antigone asked.

"What do I want? How can you even ask that? What I want is for all this bullshit to be over. I want not to have to be in hiding anymore. I want not to have to wonder at every sound from the hall if that's the police or the prince's goons coming to kick down the door. I want not to—"

"I didn't ask you what you don't want, Mr. Felton," Antigone interrupted. "I asked you what you want."

This took him aback. He was quiet for some time. Brooding, fighting down angry comebacks, trying to decide whom he was even angry at anymore. "I want to clear my name," he said at last, voice heavy with weariness. "I want it all back, back to being..." He let the thought trail off into bitterness and recriminations.

"I can't give you your old existence back, Mr. Felton," she said. She squeezed his hand and then extracted the lighter from beneath it. He did not resist her. "But I can make sure that you have some say in your future. No more running. No more hiding. No more trying to do it all on your own. We're in this together, the three of us. Okay?"

The Zippo chirped to life and a tongue of flame leapt from it. Antigone lit the candle, and flipped the still-lit Zippo back to him. Felton caught it without even looking at it and snapped it shut.

He knew he had no choice, not really. He could no more walk out on them now than he could have missed that lighter. After ten years of fighting, the combat reflexes were hard-wired into him.

"Okay," he replied at last. "I'm in. But I get to wear the secret decoder ring."

Charlie leaned in close as if confiding a secret. "You were never out," he said.

Chapter Thirteen
A Private Transgression

Helena burst in upon Himes and Stephens hunched conspiratorially over a folding banquet table that had been set up on the dais in the Hall of Audiences. A pile of dossiers was spread out on the table between them. They argued in clipped whispers.

"Yes, yes. I told you," Himes said. "She said the transfer was complete. And I have no reason to disbelieve her. I just do not agree that this means that her usefulness to us has 'officially reached its end.' She may prove particularly helpful in the matter of keeping the novices in line and easing the transition—"

"We've got company," Stephens said, without looking up. Helena had the distinct impression that he had let Himes rattle on, despite the fact that Stephens already knew she was just outside. Not that she needed another reason to dislike the man.

Himes choked off the rest of his thought. To his credit, he had the decency to show a hint of embarrassment.

"What's needed here," Stephens said, raising his voice to carry the length of the hall. "Is an example. Don't you agree, adepta?"

"I caught your little 'example' on the way here and frankly, I've had about one example too many. Somebody want to tell me what the hell this is all about?" She stormed up to the foot of the dais and kept coming.

Stephens held her eye, even as his hands carefully closed and gathered up the scattered folders. "I shouldn't think I would have to inform *you*, adepta. As of our last interview, you were still the head of chantry security. I had been relying upon you to inform *us* of breaches of security and threats to this house. I have since had cause to reconsider that reliance."

Helena started to make a sharp retort, but forced herself to calm down and return to the subject that had brought her here.

"Anise," she said. She glowered at Himes, leaning across the table and getting right up in his face. "I want to know what she did and what the hell you think *you're* doing. You can't just waltz in here and start chaining up novices and compelling others to stone them. This isn't the damned Dark Ages. This is New York, for Christsakes! I don't know how you do things back in Vienna, and I don't really care. I don't even care if she assaulted you personally. There are proper ways to handle these things. All this ends here and now, understand?" She turned upon Stephens, "You override this damned 'death sentence' you've fed to the security system, and you do it now."

"Sit down, Helena," Stephens replied, his tone icy.

She smashed her fist down on the table, sending the newly stacked dossiers fluttering. "I don't have time to sit down. I've got a novice—a member of my security team!—facing execution in the grand foyer, damn it! I don't have time for any of this. Now are you going to—"

"I said, sit down," he repeated. His voice was quiet, but the force of the words knocked her feet out from under her. There was a weight to his command, a compulsion that her body instinctively responded to as if she herself had given it the order. She collapsed awkwardly into the nearest metal folding chair.

"I don't know what the hell you're trying to pull...." she growled, immediately starting to rise again.

"If you insist on asking insubordinate questions," Stephens said, "you will at least sit still to hear their answers."

Reaching across the table, he put a hand on her shoulder, preventing her from rising. Helena raged at the uninvited contact, but resisted the temptation to take him by the arm and throw him across the room. He was purposefully trying to get under her skin; she would not take the bait. Fuming, she sank back into the chair.

"Talk," she said.

"I'm not altogether certain," he said, "why you should think you have the right to storm in here and make demands of us. You are not owed any explanation and there is no one in this investigation that is — in any way — accountable to you. I trust we understand one another?"

Helena said nothing.

"Excellent," Stephens said. "You also understand that you continue to serve in your present capacity only through the continued support and intervention of Mr. Himes and myself? To be quite frank, the standard procedure for investigating such gross violations of chantry security — a series of grisly murders, the death of an official ambassador from the Fatherhouse, not to mention the direct assault on the person of an investigator — is to immediately remove the chantry's security officer and his or her team. *Permanently* remove them. I trust that you understand and appreciate the need for such firm measures."

Helena could contain herself no longer. "That's it?! That's why you're stoning novices to death? Because they were part of the security team? Anise didn't have anything to do with any of those deaths. Why single her out? In fact, right up until a few hours ago, she was with me in the security control room, busting her butt to implement all those new protocols and profiles that you requested. She—"

Himes cleared his throat. "You may have been, ehrm, unaware of certain salient details of the novice's case. Were you aware, for instance, that she has confessed to attempting to undermine you by hacking into the chantry security system and reprogramming it to her own ends?"

Helena rolled her eyes. "Of course I know about that. *Everybody* knows about that. I brought it to the regent's attention over two years ago. The report should still be—"

"And you took no steps to stop her, to reprimand her for this treachery?" Stephens jumped in. "Even when other novices started turning up murdered?"

"Of course not! Anise didn't have anything to do with those deaths. Anise's attempts to bypass the security system were harmless. They were harmless precisely *because* we all knew about them. All the changes she entered were executed in local simulation only and then diverted to a filter for my okay before being implemented on the actual systems grid. If there was anything I didn't like, I set up some localized system crash that knocked down her terminal and wiped out the changes. A small bit of effort, but well worth it to keep a promising novice occupied with a known subterfuge, rather than looking for a new one. Plus it's always nice to have a secret transgression to hold over a subordinate should such become needed."

Himes nodded sympathetically. "It seems, however," he said, "that the novice thought to return the favor."

"What do you mean?" Helena said, suddenly alert for new danger.

"What he means," Stephens said, "is that this novice conspired to cover up certain critical security failures these last few nights—a second fire in the novice *domicilium*, for instance. Or the fact that a dangerous dark thaumaturge who had infiltrated the chantry—and attacked an investigator—was somehow allowed to escape. Or that the most wanted man in the city, the saboteur responsible for the bombing at the Empire State Building, has mysteriously disappeared from our custody.

When pressed on the point, the novice admitted to lying about these matters to protect you."

"To protect me?! That's ridiculous. Look, Stephens, Anise had nothing to do with any of those things. She—"

"She was," Himes said, "the ranking security officer on duty on the night in question. And you must admit that your own absence, under such circumstances, is somewhat... disturbing."

"I was locked in here with you two for 'questioning' the entire evening! I don't believe this...."

"But you weren't here the entire evening, were you, adepta? And even if you had been, that would still not absolve you of your responsibility in this matter. You were—excuse me—*are* the head of chantry security. You are ultimately accountable for everything that goes on within these walls."

"But Anise is not," Helena said. "If she tried to conceal what happened that night from you, she was wrong. And if she felt she had to cover it up for my sake, then that was wrong, too. And I'll deal with that. We have standard operating procedures of our own to handle such transgressions. But she certainly does not deserve—"

"You have such 'transgressions' regularly?" Stephens asked.

Helena thought she saw where this line of questioning was leading. She moved to head it off.

"We're talking about Anise," she said stubbornly. "Now, are you going to turn her loose or am I going to have to do it myself?"

"That, adepta," Himes put in, trying to defuse the situation, "would be extremely unwise."

Chapter Fourteen
What the Mirror Saw

A ntigone held the candle before her face. Her words caused the flame to flutter and jump.

"I know you're in trouble, Felton," she began uncertainly. "There are an awful lot of folks who'd sooner stake you out for the sun than look at you. But I guess I can relate to that. We are not so different, you and I. I can't help but think that what we need is just to start over. To put some mistakes behind us, and the enemies that come with them. So I guess what I'm trying to say is that I'm willing to pitch in with you guys. You've always been straight with me and, if it comes down to a fight, I know I want you—both of you—on my side. *Fide et vigilante*, I stand with you."

She touched the lit taper in her hand to the white candle on the vanity. The wick hissed and sputtered to life. An oily black smoke and the unmistakable reek of burning fat filled the tiny room.

Felton found something about the candle unsettling. It grated on the nerves. Not the smell, but something in the light that it gave off. It was muted, murky. Peering closely into the writhing flame, he realized that it was not a flame at all, but rather a flickering tongue of blood that danced atop the wick.

Antigone handed the taper to Charlie, who looked decidedly uncomfortable. He held it at arm's length as if she had just handed him a dirty diaper. "I don't... what do I say?" he whispered. "I don't even know any Latin."

"It doesn't matter," Antigone confided in his ear. "The words don't matter at all, just so long as you mean them."

"Okay, I'll give it a shot," he said. He cleared his throat. "Hell, I guess I've been pulling this bastard out of trouble ever since I've known him. And I'm coming to realize that it's probably too late to stop now. Who am I kidding? It's been too late for some time now. Don't get me wrong, I'm not nursing any illusions on that score—I know full well that when they catch up to this sorry bastard, I'm a dead man too. Just for what little I've done for him up until now.

"So I guess what I'm trying to say," Charlie continued, "is that I really don't have anything more to lose in pitching in with you two now. It's funny though. I had kind of thought that I was easing out of all this—out of the Conventicle stuff, I mean. You know, settling down. Starting a little business of my own. But it seems that it all kind of crept back up on me. The damned thing is that I'm realizing now that I'm kind of glad it did. Oh hell, listen to me. Break out the violins. Fuck it, I'm in. *Sic Semper... Fi*," he finished awkwardly.

Charlie shuffled his feet a bit, scuffing at the pattern of still-wet wax droplets on the floor. Antigone nudged him and he came back to himself. "Hmm? Oh... right," he said. He crowded past her and lit the red candle on the vanity, which also sprang to sanguine life.

"Up to you, buddy," he said, pressing the taper into Felton's hand. "All for one..."

Felton snorted and did not meet Charlie's eye. "Aw hell," he said. "I never really believed that either of you were gunning for me. Despite what the Bonespeaker said." He glanced sidelong at Antigone, but she remained silent.

"And if either of you were out to get me," he continued, "it's obvious that you're so incompetent at it that I would want to keep you around anyway. Just so when the real bad asses showed up, I'd have you guys on hand to screw things up for them. Anyway, all I'm trying to say is that you guys have already said you'd watch my back. Said it? Hell, you've both already put your sorry worm-eaten carcasses on the line for my sake. So I'd have to be a complete bastard to just walk away from you guys now."

Charlie put a hulking arm across the doorway.

"Very funny, asshole," Felton said. Then, appealing to Antigone, "You see what I have to put up with? You sure you want to sign on for this?"

She nodded. "Dead sure."

"Be careful what you wish for, Blackbird," Felton said. "The walls have ears." He bent and placed the tip of the taper to the remaining black candle. A third tongue of blood leaped from its wick.

"They also have eyes. Let all bear witness to what was said and enacted here this night," Antigone recited, taking the taper from his hand. "Let the pledge that we have sworn become the mortar on which the Conventicle is rebuilt—the flame with which it rises from its own ashes, the detritus of the past."

She touched the taper to the puddle of blood in the bottom of the basin and a flame the size of her hand leapt to life. It burned hot and white like magnesium. As she blinked her vision clear, Antigone could see that the blaze was made of three distinct flames. Just as the fire atop each of the three candles had drawn upon the blood, so the fire in the midst of the pool of blood drew upon their three flames. "It is done," she said.

Antigone dipped the fingertips of her right hand into the puddle of burning blood, careful to avoid the consuming flames. Then she traced a sign upon the face of the mirror. It was her sign, a hieroglyph. The stylized, leering face of the jackal.

She gestured for Charlie to come forward. Tentatively, he followed her example, dipping his fingers repeatedly into the blood as he sketched out a picture upon the glass. The image was the shield device familiar from the Harley Davidson logo. Emblazoned upon it were a skull and what looked like a runner of long bones, linked together in parallel, one atop the other. He stepped back to admire it, obviously quite pleased with his clumsy finger-painting.

Felton was the last to step forward. "This is silly," he muttered, but seeing that he would receive no sympathy from his fellows, he relented. He dipped one finger into the blood and with a series of deft motions, traced out the letters *Non Serviam* upon the glass.

Charlie could not have been more impressed had Felton written *Helter Skelter*. "Hey," he accused jealously. "That's Latin. Where do you get off knowing any Latin?"

"Crash course," Felton replied, thinking back to his period of captivity at the Tremere chantry. "Long story. Don't ask. Doesn't have a happy ending."

Antigone stared at the symbols etched in blood upon the mirror. It was done. Their pledge renewed. But she saw more than that in the three sanguine marks upon the glass.

She cocked her head to one side like some kind of curious bird. The bone-white avian mask only heightened the impression. With a start, she realized that she could still see her reflection, even in the red lines that streaked the mirror's surface. It was a reflection distorted by the ruddy smudges and cast in an unhealthy glow.

But it was more than that. Suddenly she realized why the reflection was bothering her so much. As she stared at the figure in the mirror, it was not the sharp avian features of the Bonespeaker mask that she saw staring back at her.

Quickly, before the image could shift and be gone again, she dipped her fingertips into the basin of blood and streaked them across the mirror. In the wide swath of red, she confirmed what she had only glimpsed before. The face before her was the face of a man, a familiar man. And the object jutting from his face was not an avian beak, but rather the butt end of a pistol.

Behind her, Charlie drew breath sharply and Felton cursed. "Hello, Mr. Graves," he muttered.

Antigone ignored them, smearing more blood across the mirror, coating it with a thin red film. As more of the reflective surface was coated, more of the grisly scene was revealed — the picture frozen in time of Adam Graves' final moments.

"I don't get it," Charlie said. "What's going on? What the hell are we seeing here?"

"The walls have ears," Felton muttered, realization dawning as he found himself once again hearing Antigone's earlier words.

"And mirrors are walls with eyes," Antigone said, "even if they are only borrowed ones. Something this traumatic doesn't happen in a vacuum. The memory of Graves' last sight is etched into the glass. Its mark is as permanent as the signs we placed here with blood and promises."

Charlie said nothing. He was obviously shaken. His eyes were fixed on the eyes of a dead man in the mirror. But he was not staring at Graves. "Who's that?" he asked.

"That's him, Graves," Felton said. "You've seen him. On the TV."

"Not him," Charlie said. He stepped forward and rubbed his hand over the mirror in a circular motion. As if he were wiping it clean of steam from the shower. "Him."

In the new swirl of red, Antigone and Felton could see clearly what Charlie had glimpsed from his angle. The face of a second man, standing in the doorway.

Felton spun and for a moment seemed confused to find the doorway empty. When he turned back to the glass however, there was the face of the stranger, staring back at him.

"Jeez, you're jumpy," Charlie said. "He's not here now. The mirror's showing us stuff things as they were when Graves—"

"I know what it's showing us," Felton snapped. "It just startled me is all. Seeing someone else standing over my shoulder. I mean, his shoulder. Oh, forget it."

"Whoever he is," Charlie said, "he didn't kill Graves. Look at him. He's just standing there. Sure, it's a little sick watching somebody blow his brains out, but it's not murder." Charlie had continued to smear the glass and had now achieved a nearly uniform coating. The coagulating fluid still ran down the pane in viscous rivulets, but the entire scene was revealed now as if the trio had been there the night Graves had died.

"Estevez," Antigone said in a quiet voice.

"You know that guy?" Felton replied.

"Eugenio Estevez. He's one of the most prominent Tremere in the city."

"So what gives?" Charlie demanded. "What's some muckety-muck Tremere bigwig doing standing in someone's bathroom doorway watching him off himself? It's just creepy. Is this the kind of thing this guy does often? Is this some kind of blood rite? Killing yourself always struck me as sort of, you know, a private moment. Why would Graves have Estevez here to witness his suicide?"

"It's not any kind of blood rite," Antigone said. "And Estevez is not some kind of Dr. Kevorkian either. No, if Estevez was ever part of some 'assisted suicide' it wouldn't have been motivated by sympathy for the suffering of others. And I bet he would have had a much more active assist."

"But it's not his hand on the trigger," Felton pointed out. "Whatever you make of Estevez's part in all this, the fact remains that Graves offed himself. End of story. And that means we're right back where we started."

"But he could still have driven Graves to do it," Charlie objected. "Maybe he had something over him."

"If Jervais knew that Graves was involved," Antigone put in, "then Estevez knew too. Jervais was Estevez's toady. His 'aide-de-camp,' as he was so fond of pointing out...."

"So Graves tipped off the Bonespeaker. Then the Bonespeaker—that is, Jervais—told Estevez. And Estevez did what? Tried to blackmail Graves?" Felton threw up his hands. "It's all circular. And all we've got to show for it is a trail of corpses."

Antigone stared into Estevez's eyes, trying to divine his motives from the dead man's remains. Sifting through blood and entrails.

She started as she saw Estevez's lips move. In silence, his reflection mouthed the words, "Goodbye, Mr. Graves."

As if in response, Graves' finger tightened on the trigger. His knuckle whitened and then Antigone found herself involuntarily ducking beneath the spray of blood and gore. A silly reflexive action. That blood had already fallen.

A silly reflexive action.

Antigone found herself thinking of Mr. Stephens and her confrontation with the astors. Of how she had squirmed under his questions as under the first touch of the rising sun. There was a note of command in his voice. A note that compelled answers, forced a response from her body, even before she could will compliance or defiance. A reflexive action.

Estevez was long accustomed to command, and was certainly powerful enough to elicit the same unthinking animal response. To condition an answer, or a reflexive act in response to only his voice. Powerful enough that he could kill without ever having to lower himself to putting his own finger upon the trigger. Antigone knew it was not easy to make even the most pliant of mortals take their own lives, but with proper conditioning, Estevez could have bypassed Graves' instinct of self-preservation. A few key words would be enough to elicit the nervous jerk of one finger and speed the bullet on its way. *Goodbye, Mr. Graves.*

As Antigone stared at the reflection of Estevez, the older Tremere smiled, fished a handkerchief from his pocket and dabbed at a spot on his sleeve. Apparently, he hadn't been quite free of the blast.

As she watched, the reflection of Estevez turned slightly, as if disturbed by a puzzling thought and stared *directly back at Antigone.* She saw his lips form around a question. "Jervais?" He stepped closer to the mirror, peering back out at her.

Her hand went instinctively to her face in alarm. She came up short against the whitened avian mask of the Bonespeaker. She knew then what Estevez was seeing: the mask of the Bonespeaker, the persona of his apprentice, Jervais.

Then the face in the mirror smiled at her, a terrible smile that Antigone felt like a gulf opening up within her. She was held by it, pinned and wriggling like a specimen for dissection. And then, somehow, Estevez saw.

"No, *not* Jervais," he mouthed. "Very curious." And Antigone found herself falling forward into the gulf of his mocking smile. Strong hands caught her from behind, before her forehead could impact the porcelain sink. But it was too late, she knew. Already too late. Estevez had somehow seen something in the mirror as well. Seen back out through it, just as Antigone, Felton and Charlie had peeked in. And in that momentary meeting of eyes, Antigone knew that they were all doomed.

"Jeez, you all right, Blackbird?" Felton said. "Antigone, listen to me! You okay? How many fingers?"

Antigone swatted him away.

"She's lost too much blood," Felton said to Charlie. "We've got to get out of here, get something into her system."

"Quit talking about me as if I'm not right here," Antigone said, pushing herself upright. "I'm okay."

"I think you must have blacked out for a minute there," Charlie said, still not relinquishing his grip upon her arm, despite her feeble efforts to dislodge him.

"Well, I'm all right now. Just give me a hand cleaning up this mess and we can get out of here."

"I'm afraid that's not going to be possible," said an unfamiliar voice. All three of them involuntarily spun to face the mirror. It was a silly reflexive response, but in this case, one that seemed justified. The mirror-man's lips moved in time to the words.

Estevez's reflection leaned casually against the door frame. Only this time one hand seemed to be resting on another support—the barrel of a shotgun. Charlie's shotgun.

But that couldn't be. Charlie's shotgun had not even been in the apartment on the night that Graves died. Charlie had brought it only this evening.

And left it leaning beside the refrigerator....

From the doorway, Estevez's voice said, "Now, if you can drag yourselves away from the mirror, we have plans for the evening."

Chapter Fifteen
Shadow Beneath the Door

Dorfman glanced at his watch for perhaps the tenth time, clearly uneasy. He sat perched upon the corner of the ponderous writing table that dominated the center of Meerlinda's private library—a pose of studied nonchalance. But Sturbridge could see his agitation. They had been waiting for nearly half an hour now. She took it that it was not their hostess's habit to be late for her appointments.

Sturbridge occupied herself with pacing the length of the heavily laden stacks. She tried hard not to run her hands along the leather spines, which had gone brittle and glossy with age and frequent handling. She could see already that she was going to fail miserably at the effort and wished she had thought to bring gloves.

She murmured quietly to herself, as if counting off the number of volumes or reciting their titles. In actuality, she was committing the collection to memory—their names, their exact positions—for later perusal. She stopped short, a soft squeal of delight escaping her, despite her best efforts to muffle it.

"I do wish you'd sit down," Dorfman called irritably. "The councilor hates people pawing through her things and you'd hate to be caught at it when she does arrive."

"You don't understand," Sturbridge said. "This is a Pythagoras! An *original* Pythagoras. Not a modern translation.

Not some Renaissance reconstruction. Not even an ancient Roman knock-off of the Greek text. An *original* Pythag—"

"Yes, yes" Dorfman interrupted. "I'm sure the councilor's collection is very impressive. But this isn't really the time or the place. If I were you, I'd be giving some serious thought to just what the hell you're going to say to her. Once she finally gets here."

Sturbridge sighed and tore herself away from the stacks. "I'm going to tell her the truth," she said. "If necessary, I'll give her a demonstration of what I know and exactly how I know it."

"Do you think that's wise?" he asked. "I mean, sure I didn't kill you outright when you pulled that stunt on me. But then again I was under orders to bring you back here alive. The councilor is under no such constraints."

She smiled. "Is that why? I wondered. Still, the councilor needs to know what has happened. Have you sent back word about any of this yet? About the Children? About Eva?"

"Who am I going to entrust with a message like that?" He shook his head. "My ass is on the line here too, Aisling. Don't screw this up."

His sudden vehemence took her aback. "Look, I didn't ask for any of this either, okay? I'm the victim here, remember? And I'm doing my best to figure this thing out, just like you are. So how about you give me a break?"

"Sorry," he muttered, glancing distractedly at the door. And, she noted, not sounding terribly sincere.

"And I don't know what you're so worried about," she accused. "If Meerlinda doesn't buy it, you just throw me to the wolves and walk away. You tell her that I've cracked. That the pressures of holding off the Sabbat all those years were just too much to handle for 'one so young and inexperienced.' You file your reports and you move on."

Instead of shock or protest, he said simply, "Let's hope it doesn't come to that."

They sat in silence, each brooding upon the few unappealing options that remained to them. And upon what each of them was willing to betray to get out of this mess.

As her mind raced through a labyrinth of dead-end passages, Aisling found her eyes drawn back to the door, tracing each of the lines of the grain, each knot in the wood. As if the accidental pattern that nature had etched upon it were somehow a map to the treacherous inner maze she wandered. Gradually, she became aware that something was wrong.

She could not put her finger on it at first. Something about the door. About the pattern of light and shadow playing upon its surface. And around it.

And then she saw it. The unmistakable shadow just beneath the crack of the door. A shadow that spoke of someone standing patiently just outside. Listening.

Without a word, she took Dorfman by the elbow and gestured towards the doorway with her other hand.

"What is it now?" he snapped, irritated at being dragged from his thoughts. He followed the line of her arm. "Oh."

Sturbridge gestured for silence. Dorfman nodded his understanding and slid quietly from his perch atop the desk.

Creeping towards the doorway, Sturbridge was just reaching out for the handle when she cried out. Dorfman, circling towards the other side of the door, rolled his eyes, throwing up his hands wide in a gesture that clearly said *so much for silence*. When he saw Sturbridge stumble, however, his manner changed in an instant. He rushed over to her.

Sturbridge felt a hot piercing pain at her heel, as if she had trodden on broken glass. She craned around backwards, peering over her shoulder and hitching up the trailing skirts of the black novice robes. There was an angry twist of red at the back of her ankle, just above her heel. A shimmering ruby serpent, no longer than the breadth of her hand, clung to her tenaciously.

With a sickening feeling in her stomach, she shook her leg, trying to dislodge the viper. But the serpent only coiled itself intimately around her ankle.

"Hold still!" Dorfman ordered, stooping and catching hold of her leg. He made a grab for the writhing serpent, but it slid through his grasp. He cursed, his hand coming away covered with blood.

For a moment Sturbridge had the unsettling impression that the snake had actually squished right through Dorfman's fingers, as if it were no more substantial than a viscous ribbon of blood. But that was clearly impossible for any creature of flesh and bone.

She felt lightheaded. It was all she could do to keep herself upright. "Venom?" she muttered aloud to no one in particular. Dorfman looked up distractedly and the serpent again slipped his grasp. Sturbridge knew that she, like all of her kind, was immune to most varieties of poison and venom—a side-effect of her near-death state. This conclusion had been well documented and born out through extensive experimentation. Something was terribly wrong here.

Looking down, she was certain that the serpent was much smaller than it had been a moment ago. Could the pain, blood loss and toxins be playing tricks with her perceptions? "Shrinking," she slurred. She needed to sit down, she thought, seconds before she slumped to the floor in a heap.

"Aisling!" Dorfman barked. Both of his hands were covered to the wrists in blood and still he could get no purchase on the elusive creature. He knew he was running out of time.

He could clearly see what Sturbridge, at this point, only suspected. The serpent was markedly smaller. And Dorfman knew why. He could see the disturbing bulge running up the back of Aisling's calf, just under the skin. The tiny predator had gone deep and was already pushing up through the disused course of an artery.

"Hold on," he said. "This may hurt a little." He pressed one knee down onto the back of her calf and knelt down upon it with all his weight. Applying pressure, trying to pinch off the path to her heart.

He cupped his already bloodied hands and ran them over one another as if lathering them with soap. A pinprick of light appeared within the hollow of his palm—a flicker than soon grew to a tongue of flame.

There was a sizzle of seared flesh as he locked his hand around her ankle. Sturbridge lurched and kicked out at him, suddenly aware of the presence of a more ancient and deadly enemy, the touch of fire. Something primordial and unreasoning took hold of her, struggling for control.

Chapter Sixteen
An Unfortunate Introduction

F elton started threateningly towards the figure blocking the doorway, but Antigone held him back with an arm across his chest.

"You're not going to believe this," she said to Estevez, "but we were just talking about you."

"How charming," he replied. "I hope I am not interrupting, but I've been waiting for you for some time now. Ever since I realized that Jervais was not coming back, and why."

"You'd do well to think about that 'why' part," Felton said. "Jervais got himself killed for screwing with us...."

"I assure you, Mr. Felton," Estevez paused to let the fact sink in that he was aware of exactly who they were, "that I am not here to... what was your colorful idiom? Ah yes, 'screw with you.' I am here to make you a simple business proposition. One that it is in your best interest to accept. Now, Ms. Baines, please do take off that ridiculous mask. I was, perhaps, overly indulgent of Jervais and his amateur theatrics. It is a bad habit that I have repented of."

Antigone's hands went reflexively to the mask and she had removed it before it even occurred to her to question Estevez's command. She cursed herself for her instinctual obedience to Tremere authority. It was a habit that had been bred into her over seventy years of unflagging service to the Pyramid. Now, she realized, it was a potentially lethal liability.

"What do you mean, you've been waiting for us?" Felton demanded. "You've been watching us the whole time? Following us?"

"No, nothing of the sort. I have been waiting for you because, a few nights ago, when Mr. Graves here met his untimely end, I caught a glimpse of a face in that mirror. A face wearing a ridiculous bird mask. Even at the time, it startled me, puzzled me. Of course, I assumed it was Jervais in his comical Bonespeaker getup. But tonight I realized it could not have been Jervais. Jervais was already dead. It had to be someone else, wearing his mask, standing in front of this very mirror. And that meant—"

"That meant that whoever killed Jervais was on your tail," Felton said, following the chain of thought to its logical conclusion. "But you didn't know who that was."

"Oh, I had some strong guesses," Estevez replied. "What I did not know was *when* Jervais's killer would come to stand in front of this mirror. So I watched and waited. And here you are."

"Sounds like an awful lot of trouble to go through just to get yourself killed," Felton said.

"I quite agree," Estevez replied. "For me it was no trouble at all. But when I think of all the wasted effort—all the pointless stumbling about that you have been doing... why, it's a wonder any of you've lived long enough to make this meeting."

"You said something about a deal?" Charlie interrupted.

"Ah yes. You do come right to the point, Mr. Rosetti. An excellent quality."

Felton looked at Charlie. He couldn't remember ever having heard his fellow conspirator's last name before. He kept stretching at it, trying to get it to fit over the familiar hulking frame of his companion.

"The deal is very simple really," Estevez said. "You return with me to the Maupassant Room. There is a circle of apportation waiting for you there that will take you all out of the country. Your departure will be instantaneous and untraceable."

Charlie looked at Antigone. "Can he do that?" Felton asked in a whisper.

Estevez laughed aloud. "My dear Mr. Felton, of course I can do that. Once established, and properly tested, the apportation diagram is one hundred percent safe and reliable. Why, even a novice could do it. Is that not so, Ms. Baines?"

Antigone started to say something and then stopped, choking on the hot rush of shame. She might have blushed, had her blood still flowed along its accustomed pathways. *This* novice could do no such thing, and Estevez knew it.

"Well, can he?" Felton demanded, not trusting Estevez's word on anything.

Reluctantly, Antigone nodded.

"There, that's settled then," Estevez said, straightening. "We will return to the Maupassant Room at once."

"That's not a deal," Charlie said.

Estevez looked startled. "I beg your pardon."

"A deal means that you give something and you get something. You told us what you're selling. Now, what's in it for you?"

"I should have thought," Estevez said, "that would be obvious. Your job is merely to leave town and forget that any of this ever happened."

"Just like that?" Felton demanded. "Just forget about it? I'm afraid it's not that easy."

"It is that easy, Mr. Felton. No one is going to dog your steps for the rest of your existence to check up on you. To ensure that you have, in fact, forgotten. All I am asking from you is the promise that you will do what I ask and put all of this behind you. Is that so much to ask? Surely that is what all of us want at this point—to start afresh."

Felton shook his head. "Nope, we already made a promise. A promise to make our stand together, right here."

"And you will be together, all of you," Estevez explained with thinning patience. "I am offering you an opportunity to make a stand that will mean something. If you remain here, you will be hunted down—by the prince, by the chantry, by the mortal authorities. What do any of these people care about your stand? What can it possibly mean to them? In their eyes, you are already judged and condemned. Better to start over somewhere else. Somewhere where you have a fighting chance."

Felton looked from Antigone to Charlie, but neither would meet his eye. "I don't believe this," he said. "You guys aren't actually considering this? We've tracked this mess back to this bastard and it's going to end here. Are you forgetting that this guy tried to kill the prince? He blew up the damned Empire State Building. Jervais found out about it and decided to take the opportunity to set you up as the mad bomber, Antigone. And then—"

"I assure you, Mr. Felton," Estevez said, "that I did not blow up any building."

That brought Felton up short. "What do you mean, you didn't blow up any building? You're the one who told Graves about it. That's why Graves had to die, because he was the last link back to you. And it would have worked too, if not for the fact that Antigone somehow summoned up the image of Graves' final moments from the only other witness at the scene of the crime—the mirror."

"Be that as it may," Estevez said. "I did not blow up any building. I know nothing of demolitions and, frankly, I find such methods of problem-solving unsophisticated. If I were going to resort to such direct methods, I would at least have the courtesy to confront the prince face to face so that he might know who had killed him."

"All right, I'll bite," Charlie said. "Who blew up the building?"

"That's the first sensible question any of you have asked since I arrived," Estevez said. "It is also one that I am not going to answer."

Felton started to protest, but Estevez silenced him with a raised hand.

"There are forces at work here that are greater than either of us, and the sooner you resolve yourselves to this fact, the better off we'll all be."

"No deal," Felton said flatly. "The fact remains that you set me up, and—"

"I believe you mean to say that Jervais set you up. Or, more precisely, that Jervais set Ms. Baines up. You have already avenged that insult and you know that I had nothing to do with it. Surely you see that it would be far better for me personally if none of you were ever involved in this. For this same reason, I tried to keep Jervais sheltered from knowing anything about these events, but Mr. Graves injudiciously tipped our hand."

"Still not buying it," Felton said. "If that were so, why would you tell Graves about it? By that reasoning, Graves would be just another liability."

It was Charlie that answered him. "Unless, of course, Graves had some other part to play in all this and got dealt in on a 'need to know' basis."

"What kind of part to play?" Felton demanded. "You saying Graves set that bomb?"

"No. But every deal needs a backer. And Graves' outfit, Cyanight, has a lot of financial clout to throw around. And a lot to gain by this attack."

"Are you kidding? Cyanight took a beating over this. Graves was all over the news for days, apologizing for... shit."

"Gentlemen," Estevez soothed, "we really don't have time for this. Suffice it to say that Cyanight had a significant financial stake in the bombing. Besides the overwhelming amount of free publicity they picked up, as Mr. Felton pointed out, I believe you will find that their chief competitor was headquartered in the building and suffered an unprecedented and destabilizing loss in the disaster. So, now that your morbid curiosity is sated, may we go?"

"One question left," Charlie said. "Where do you come into all of this? I mean, what's in it for you? Graves and his company stand to make a mint. Jervais thinks he's striking a blow against the prince and disposing of a Tremere rival at the same time. But why are you involved?"

"My dear Mr. Rosetti, you have gotten it quite backwards again. I have nothing to gain here. I did not even particularly want the explosion to happen. I am merely a facilitator, a catalyst. I bring people together. Like you three, for example. What they do once they get together is really none of my affair. Nor is it my responsibility. Mr. Graves had the ready cash. Jervais, as you know, had certain militant contacts—no offense to the present company intended. It was, perhaps, an *unfortunate* introduction."

At last Antigone spoke. "Jervais and Graves paid for that introduction with their lives."

"And I intend," Estevez said pointedly, "that they should be the last ones to do so. However, you are not making things any easier for me. I ask you, again, will you or will you not return with me to the Maupassant Room?"

"You don't feel any remorse about this?" Antigone mused aloud. "Over what you set in motion? Jervais was your pupil, your protégé. He idolized you. You lived and worked together every day for years. And you can just write him off like that?"

"Write him off like what, Ms. Baines? Jervais is dead. There is nothing I can do to change that. I can, however, if I keep my wits about me and do not fall into melancholy, keep the rest of us alive. Is that so monstrous? Is that somehow disrespectful of the dead? The duty of the living is to live. Nothing more, even for those of us whose lives are somewhat unnatural. I cannot speak to the duties of the dead. I would hope that once I find myself in that austere company, that I am not charged with visiting reproaches against those that are still among the living. With keeping them from doing what is right and necessary. Now I, for one, am going. Are you coming, or do you remain here?"

Antigone shook her head sadly. "I would not presume to speak for anybody else," she said. "If they would go with you, I release them from the oaths they have sworn. They can go in good faith and start over somewhere else."

"But you're not going," Felton said. He drew himself up. "So I don't see any more need to stand around here talking to this bozo. Charlie?"

"No deal, Mr. Estevez," Charlie said.

Chapter Seventeen
Helena's Choice

"It is really very simple, adepta," Himes explained. "Surely you can understand our position. We cannot condone such blatant breaches of security, especially during the course of an official inquiry. What message would that send to the novices of this house, hmm? The will of the Fatherhouse, the power and authority of the Pyramid, these will neither be challenged nor thwarted. I trust that we understand one another."

"So you're going to stone an innocent novice into torpor and leave her out for the sun? For what? To keep from looking bad in front of the locals? Is that what you're telling me? Do you realize how stupid and backwards—"

"Carefully," Himes warned. Helena ignored him.

"I've already told you that Anise wasn't involved in any of those things. She's one of the good ones—she's loyal, she works hard—"

"All of this is beside the point," Stephens interrupted. "Your security team screwed up again, and someone has to be held accountable. Now, if you know of anyone else who would like to stand up and take responsibility for your team's shortcomings…?"

"Fuck you," Helena retorted. "If you bastards hadn't been giving me the third degree the whole night, we wouldn't be in this mess. In fact — and I don't think I'm going to go way out on a limb here to say so — but my guess is that if you insist on trying to kill off my security team, things are going to get dramatically worse. Now, how about you release Anise and get the hell out of my way so that I can do my job?"

Stephens sighed and steepled his fingers, rubbing at the bridge of his nose. "Okay," he said.

Helena choked back an angry retort, stunned by his unexpected acquiescence. "Okay?" she parroted back to him. She looked back and forth between the two men, but Himes would not meet her gaze.

"Okay, I agree," Stephens said. "I'll let Anise go. But I need someone to make an example of. Someone to help demonstrate that this isn't a game we're playing here. In short, what I need is someone to take her place. Now, you give me a name, and a formal report to back it up, and we let Anise go."

Helena's mind flashed immediately to the names of four other novices that were more expendable than her trained security officer. Then she cursed out loud, angry at Stephens for this offer that was no offer. Angry at herself for how quickly she was willing to sell out the novices entrusted to her care.

"Shall I take that as a no?" Stephens asked. "Well, it's your choice to make. You are the head of security; I leave the matter in your… capable hands. If you choose to save your novice, save her. If you choose to condemn her, that is your business. But in future, save us these little theatrical tirades. We also have quite a bit of work to do and it is getting late. So if there is nothing further…"

"Himes," Helena said. She jerked her head towards him, but her eyes never left Stephens'.

"Yes, adepta? There was something more?" Himes asked.

"You said that I get to choose; I choose Himes."

Himes rose sputtering to his feet, but Stephens laid a hand on his arm, gesturing for him to sit back down. "Out of the question," Stephens said. He never even looked up. His attention had already shifted back to the scattered pile of dossiers. He opened one at random and began to skim down the page. "Has to be someone local, one of the novices, perhaps. Here we go. How about this one? Anselm, Peter, Novice, Fifth Circle. Says here he had access to both the renegade and the prisoner. That should do nicely. Any objections?"

"Brother Anselm is acting master of novices in Johanus's absence," Helena replied in clipped tones. "Making a scapegoat out of him will only increase the panic among the novices."

Stephens didn't even wait until she had stopped speaking. He slapped the folder closed and slid it towards Himes. He opened another. "Jacqueline," he read. "Novice, Third Circle. Apprenticed to Foley, Johnston, Secondus."

Himes cleared his throat and then mumbled something low to Stephens.

"Ah, yes. *Another* of the victims." He slapped the folder closed and pushed it in the direction that *Anselm, Peter* had taken. "It's getting to where you need a scorecard just to keep up with all the murdered novices around here."

"Look, this isn't getting us anywhere," Helena objected. "Can't you just—"

"Jervais, Novice, Third Circle," Stephens interrupted. "Exemplary service record. Wonder how a nice boy like you ended up in a place like this." He looked expectantly at Helena, but she didn't meet his eye.

"No objections?" Stephens asked. "No impassioned defense of his character? No reason that he is somehow essential to the continued well-being of the chantry?"

"Jervais is missing," Helena muttered miserably. "AWOL since night before last. He's not in the chantry."

Stephens' eyes flashed rage, but instead of lashing out, he carefully closed the folder and, with excruciating slowness, slid it over to Himes. The room had fallen silent. The minutes ticked by as he calmly shuffled through the remaining folders, glancing at the contents of each until he found the one he wanted.

This one he slid across the table, not towards Himes, but to Helena. It lay untouched between them like an accusation that could neither be addressed nor tactfully withdrawn.

"Helena, Adepta," Stephens said. He barely kept the note of anger in check. "Head of chantry security. You take Anise's place and she walks. No questions asked."

Helena did not lift her gaze from the manila folder.

"We'll keep her safe," Himes said, eager to reassure. "Make sure she comes through this all right. You have my word."

Helena snorted. "Your word."

But Stephens heard the quaver of doubt in her voice and pounced. "All of them. The entire security team. We'll have to bend the rules a little, but we'll see that they all come through this. That they're quietly transferred out to other chantries. You can save them, Helena. All of them."

Helena was silent a long while. She was acutely aware of every little sound in the room. The metallic squeak of Himes craning forward in his folding chair. The rustle of Stephens regathering dossiers and the sharp tap on the tabletop as he aligned them.

Her voice, when it came was low and rumbled with barely suppressed threat. "You bastards," she spat. "You absolute bastards." She turned her back on them and stormed down from the dais.

"If you need time to think things over, adepta," Himes called after her, "I'm sure that we could wait until first thing tomorrow evening for your answer." He nudged Stephens.

"Yes, of course," Stephens agreed, his voice conciliatory and smooth as a viper. Already he knew that he had won. "Tomorrow evening then. Goodnight, Helena."

Helena did not even pause in the doorway. Over her shoulder she snarled, "Kill the bitch, then, for all I care," and slammed the door behind her.

Chapter Eighteen
Moonlight Through Glass

"You can't be serious," Estevez said. "I'm offering you a way out. One that costs you nothing and with no strings attached."

"Way I see it," Felton said, "is that we're doing you a favor. We leave town. We never mention this—specifically, your part in this—to anyone. You get off scot-free and don't even have to skip town. So what's in it for us?"

"What's in it for you, Mr. Felton, is that I don't incapacitate you and turn you over to the prince."

"Maybe you do, and maybe you don't," Felton replied. "That's your line. But the way I see it, there's three of us and only one of you. So maybe we just knock you out and turn your stinking carcass over to the prince."

"Um, Felton…" Antigone tried to interject.

If he heard her, he gave no sign of it. Instead, he advanced upon the open doorway.

"And why would the prince possibly be interested in me?" Estevez asked, storm clouds gathering in the lines of his face.

"Because you engineered this whole damned mess and tried to burn him to ash in the process!" Felton shouted. "You brought Graves and Jervais together, knowing that they would find a 'mutual interest'—knowing full well what that interest would be and what would come of it. For all I know, you were even the one to point out to Jervais that this might be an opportune time to dispose of the potential rival he had in Antigone."

"A fascinating little conjecture, I'm sure," Estevez replied calmly. "But I am uncertain on one small point: Why would the prince believe such wild tales from such—and I trust you will pardon my saying so—disreputable characters? Perhaps you simply do not know Calebros as well as I do. I think back with great fondness to the evenings of pleasant social diversions that we shared before his... unfortunate accident. I think you will find him a very practical man. I tell you this frankly—even if he were inclined to give any shred of credence to your fables, he would still have to have you destroyed. He really has no choice in this matter. His people and his reputation demand it. I trust we understand one another?"

"I'll tell you what I 'understand,'" Felton began, closing on Estevez. But he was interrupted by a sudden jarring impact. He rebounded from the open doorway as if it were a solid wall. Shaking his head to clear it, Felton started forward again. Had Estevez blindsided him with something? The air in the doorway had turned translucent, and was rapidly swimming towards opaqueness.

"What the hell?" Felton put out a hand and it met resistance in the open doorway. It was as if he had bumped into a pane of foggy glass. He put both hands against it and rattled it. It was solid. He spread his arms wide, feeling for the barrier's edges, but he could detect no gap and no seam where it met the doorjamb.

He also noticed that it was getting harder to make out Estevez's outline through the barrier. Its surface had grown bright, reflective. By the time he had finished his initial probings, Felton was staring at his own reflection.

He turned a questioning glance back towards Antigone. "Is this some kind of blood magic?"

Antigone shrugged. She knew she was out of her league here. Her raids into the thaumaturgic arts had carried away few spoils. A theoretical knowledge of the basics with little practical success in applying them. The effort was far more humiliating than productive.

Her one success along these lines had come only too recently, and arguably too late. In desperation, she had invoked an imperfectly understood hermetic diagram to try to slow down the pursuing astor. Her breakthrough, however, proved to be a Pyrrhic one. The diagram had turned out to be a forbidden dark thaumaturgic rite. Because of this unwitting trespass into the dark arts, she now found herself exiled from her peers, her order and her home.

Estevez was a reminder to her of what she had lost—of the promise that the Tremere hierarchy had dangled in front of her, just out of reach, for seventy years. He was successful, influential and powerful—not only in his position as one of the most respected Tremere in the city, but also in the arcane might he could marshal to his defense. Or, she thought, to the detriment of her and her companions.

"Look." It was Charlie's voice that interrupted her thoughts. He was pointing towards the erstwhile doorway. On its mirrored surface, the three sanguine marks that each of them had painted above the vanity in blood were now clearly visible.

Antigone immediately looked over towards the vanity, but saw that the mirror there had faded. The area now was only an unadorned stretch of wall. At the same moment, she became aware of a shift in the darkened interior of the room. A pale light was shining down upon her from directly overhead. Not the harsh glare of an artificial light, but the soft luminescence of moonlight. Glancing up, she saw that a skylight now dominated the low ceiling.

She felt a moment of vertigo. It was as if the whole room had suddenly listed to one side—the doorway becoming the mirror, the mirror becoming the opposite wall and the ceiling becoming the doorway. She squinted her eyes, but the room refuse to realign itself. It was as if the entire room had suddenly twisted along three different axes.

Antigone felt as if she were going to be sick. It was not a feeling she had experienced in many years, at least not in the decades since the majority of her internal organs had atrophied and shriveled away to dried husks.

Except for my heart, she thought, hearing the echoes of a distant, mocking laughter, catching a hint of an elusive jackal-grin. *I have it on good authority that my heart has been carefully, methodically preserved.*

Antigone knew a final reckoning was awaiting her at the hand of the leering jackal-headed guardian of the dead. She had mocked him one time too many with her lethal game of ledges, with her theatrical flirting with death and then dancing away again. When they last parted, Anubis had released her so that she might return to face the judgment of her peers.

She was beginning to suspect that he hadn't done her a favor.

She had been judged by her own kind, all right. She had systematically failed, first the representatives of Vienna, and then Sturbridge, Helena and Jervais in turn.

And now, it seemed, she had found only another judge in Estevez.

She felt the unblinking scrutiny of the moon, shining down upon her. And even that was wrong, a lie. She knew there was another story of apartments directly above this floor. There was no way that she could be seeing the open sky just on the other side of this ceiling.

From beyond the looking glass, Estevez's voice broke in upon her despondent musings. "I had hoped," he said, "that we could have reached an agreement and parted amicably. There was really never any need for you to die. If the truth were known, I would have far preferred for you to accept my offer. I would even have adjusted your memories myself and then sent you off to my overseas estates to live in comfort. But you were too proud or too stubborn or too stupid to accept my generous—"

"Wait a minute. Who said anything about 'adjusting memories'?" Felton cut in.

"It's no use quibbling over terms you have already turned down," Estevez replied. "I was quite forthright about the deal. You leave the country; you forget everything. I'm sure you would have been quite happy serving in my Viennese vineyards. Yes, I'm certain it would have been the happiest time any of you ever remembered."

"Ask me again why I don't bargain with the Tremere," Felton said disgustedly. He cast an accusatory glance towards Antigone, remembering their own deadly game of 'negotiations' when he had first sought sanctuary at the chantry house.

"But all that is moot now," Estevez said. "As you seem intent on making trouble for me, your would-be benefactor, I have repented of my earlier decision to turn you over to the prince. You will die here, I think. Tonight. Or rather, this morning."

Antigone felt a chill and her gaze went again to the skylight. The moon stared down at her contentedly, as it glided into the west. But she could not help thinking of the fate that awaited all of them when the sun rose to take its place.

Chapter Nineteen
Her Head Full of Thunder and Cotton

Strike. Scrape. Slough.

The sound came to Sturbridge, faint but steady, from far ahead down the coal-dark corridor. It was not an inviting sound.

Something struck a resounding blow against the little coffin-shaped door behind her and it leapt open, crashing against the wall and rebounding.

Framed in the opening, Sturbridge caught a momentary glimpse of the massive rust-red paw that had struck the blow and that was enough for her. She picked up her skirts and careened headlong down the passage.

Within minutes, her arms, stretched before her, were already badly battered. She strained to pick out the sounds of pursuit despite her head full of thunder and cotton. It was so dark that Sturbridge would not have been aware of the roughhewn stone walls at all were it not for the numerous twists and forks in the passage that brought their presence crashing home to her.

With growing apprehension, she realized that she was both tiring and slowing. She stumbled more frequently and once pitched entirely to the gravel floor. It was as she scrambled to regain her feet that she first noticed the bones.

Clutching at the wall to pull herself up, she found that, instead of finding any purchase on the vertical surface, her hand continued further into darkness. She flailed and caught herself, realizing as she did so that she was elbow deep in a recessed niche in the wall's face. Something rolled beneath her hand.

Sturbridge recoiled, thinking of snakes, rats, spiders and a half dozen other unpleasantries that waited in dark places for the unwary to extend a groping hand. There was the unmistakable sound of something stirring just within the recess. She stood frozen, afraid to withdraw her hand or even to move as it drew closer.

She jumped as something clattered to the floor—bouncing, then settling again. Sturbridge could feel the weight of it roll right up against her foot. She did not reach down to pick it up. Nor did she need to see the object that lay there to know what it was. She had heard the sound of its falling, striking, settling— the hollow, musical sound of each impact. She thought of an ivory flute she had owned as a child. Sturbridge clutched at this comforting (if false) image, bearing it before her like a shield as she edged away from the niche and the tattered remains it held.

She moved more slowly now, more deliberately. Her eyes squinted into the darkness, trying to pick out the outline of other recesses in the walls to either side. She could barely make out the walls themselves. As the surging panic of the Beast receded a pace, she realized two things almost at the same moment. First, there was no longer any sound of pursuit. Second, she was hopelessly lost.

The silence made the darkness thicker. Sturbridge tried to concentrate, but her thoughts could find no purchase upon the shifting foundation of silence and darkness. She knew that in the old tales, when the hero was lost in a labyrinth he would turn around, put one hand to the wall and, never breaking contact, follow it back to the entrance. Sturbridge was none too anxious to run her hand along these walls.

Her mind would not focus on the task at hand. Her thoughts kept returning to her awful discovery. Two equally appalling possibilities tugged at her. Her first thought was that she had stumbled upon some terrible secret. Someone had dragged a corpse through the little coffin-shaped door, down the maze of twisting passages and hidden it here in the dark recesses of the niche. If that were the case, there was certainly foul play here, and most probably murder. Why else would someone go to such lengths to hide a body?

The second possibility had been trying to break through for some time now. Sturbridge had been carefully guarding her thoughts from it, but her resolve was faltering. What if this were not some isolated occurrence? What if the little door off the churchyard was not unaccustomed to receiving the dead? What if she were in a vast crypt, and the entire length of every hallway in this sprawling maze of passageways was honeycombed with niches holding the teeming ranks of the dead? The thought was predatory. It scratched at the edges of her mind, impatient to claw its way in.

A familiar sound broke in upon her conjecture. Its regular rhythm was like an anchor. Sturbridge realized that this sound had never left her since she had first entered these tunnels. Even in her wild flight, its rhythm had been there, infiltrating the pounding of her feet, giving them their pace. It lurked just beneath the surface, like an undertow, invisible, but mirroring the crashing of waves above.

Strike, scrape, slough.

She found herself moving forward again, gravitating towards the sound. She followed it through seemingly endless twisting passages. She did not pause to consider at branchings in the corridor. Sometimes she wondered if a turning just taken was actually bringing her closer to or farther from the noise, but she did not turn back. She rode the sound through the darkness, not noticing that she no longer stumbled or even grazed the walls.

Soon she noticed a hint of a light ahead. As she drew closer, Sturbridge was not at all comforted to find that she could now clearly make out the line of the walls at either hand. It was not long before an even greater level of detail was revealed. Sturbridge kept her eyes locked straight ahead, trying not to notice the regular dark patches running the entire length of the walls.

Only the corners, branches and turnings seemed to be free of these dark scars. Every once in a while, the light would glitter upon something metallic within a midnight recess, but Sturbridge quickened her pace and did not investigate further.

Other details soon became apparent. The walls themselves seemed to be covered with writings: symbols, pictograms, runes, letters, script. Some of the messages were painted upon the walls, others scratched into their surface. There was surely light enough now to make out some of the inscriptions, if Sturbridge had paused to carefully examine them. She did not, for fear of examining the dark gaps that punctuated those sentences.

There was something tugging at the corners of her perception, and Sturbridge did not like its familiar groping. To distract herself, she began to count the paces between each branching. Unfortunately, in doing so she became increasingly aware of the very thing she was trying to ignore. She noticed that the darkened openings were spaced regularly, about two paces apart. In fact, she found her footsteps falling in time with their rhythm:

One, two, niche. Four, five, niche. Seven, eight, niche. Ten, eleven, turn. One, two, niche…

Soon she found herself just counting niches instead of paces:

One, step, step, two, step, step, three, step, step, turn, step, step. One, step, step…

Superimposed on this rhythm was the steady *strike, scrape, slough,* keeping perfect time, drawing her ever closer.

From the corner of her eye, she could see things beginning to come apart, her weakly lit world unraveling before the advances of the dim and dancing light. Melting into shadow as she passed.

She felt unreal, without weight or substance. Like a flickering light playing about midnight crevices of sinister import.

From somewhere beneath the surface of the rhythm of the dance, she could feel other sounds pulling at her. They came to her from a great distance, from the recesses of the vast labyrinth of passages: the plink of falling water, the scrabble of tiny clawed feet, the whistle of wind through bone, the banging of a door swinging open and shut, open and shut. She heard a moan begin, low and far away. Her pace quickened. The noise rose in pitch and intensity becoming a howl. Sturbridge broke into a run.

She tore around a corner and came suddenly, blindingly upon the source of the light. Sturbridge tried to halt, but skidded upon the loose gravel of the floor. The howl that seemed to pursue her twisted into a cry and she fell heavily over the lantern which lay nearby, overturning it and sending oil everywhere. Flame reached out for her.

She came to rest lying on her stomach, staring up at the stooped figure of a man. The man had his back to Sturbridge, but she could see that he was wearing black novice robes, identical to her own. The stranger could not have been two paces away.

At the sound of the commotion, he straightened. His shovel caught the light as it came up. It held a full measure of gravel and grave dirt.

Sturbridge felt sharp hot pain rush up and over her back. She smelled burnt hair. The howl again broke from his lips with redoubled force.

She curled, like a piece a parchment held too close to a candle. She tore at her robes, trying to free herself. She called out to the novice for help.

He stood directly over her now, oblivious to the fact that he might well be caught in the deadly flames as she rolled and thrashed. His cowl had fallen back and Sturbridge was close enough that she could see the flames reflected in the old monk's sunken eyes.

Sturbridge screamed as the darkness descended upon her. The last thing she saw was the old monk's face above her. The fire transformed that face into a bleached landscape of sharp angles and shadowed niches—a hollowed-out skull.

But then the light shifted, the face softened. Sturbridge found herself poring over the labyrinth of wrinkles that crisscrossed the monk's features. She knew she must somehow trace the lines back to the small coffin-shaped door. Dorfman would surely be looking for her. She would probably be called upon to explain her behavior to the councilor.

The last thing Sturbridge heard was the familiar *slough* of a shovel shifting its load of grave dirt. Then the earth rained down upon her and she sank into the embracing oblivion.

Chapter Twenty
Liberation by Electrocution

There was something about that moon, its outline as it hung just overhead, that was ominous. It put Antigone in mind of another celestial orb that must soon be putting in its most unwelcome appearance.

"This is bullshit," Felton said. He lowered a shoulder and crashed into the mirrored pane that blocked the exit. It rattled, but held fast, sending him staggering back a few steps. He recovered his composure as best he could under the circumstances. "Okay, very funny, asshole," he called. "Now how about you just knock this shit off and let us out of here before somebody gets his feelings hurt."

"I'm afraid not, Mr. Felton," Estevez's voice came from beyond the door. "You have made your decision and now you must live with its consequences. But perhaps 'live' is not the word I'm looking for here."

"That's it," Felton replied. He hauled off and threw a punch at the wall just to the right of the doorway. Had it been a person standing in the path of that blow, it would have crumpled bone. As it was, Felton's fist buried itself wrist-deep in the drywall. A cloud of powdery gray dust billowed out.

He swore with enthusiasm.

"As Mr. Felton is no doubt discovering, the warding with which I have sealed off your little cell forms a complete circuit.

Further efforts along these lines will meet with just as little result—unless, of course, you take into consideration the odd chance that you will strike the plumbing or wiring. Either of these occurrences will, no doubt, make the brief period of your confinement even less pleasant."

Felton managed to extract his fist, realizing that his outburst could well have resulted in a quick liberation by means of electrocution. Or worse, the slow release of a burst pipe and eventual death by drowning.

"So now what?" Felton demanded. "I suppose now you rush off to carry out your nefarious plan to take over Gotham City, leaving us here in the clutches of your ingenious death trap."

"Hmm?" Estevez replied, distracted. "Oh, I see. But no, actually. You are quite correct that I have pressing duties elsewhere, but they will keep for a while longer. What I do now is jiggle your perspective a bit. By realigning your window on the outside world, I think I may be able to find you a nice sunny day somewhere. Wouldn't that be nice? Ah, to feel the sun on my face again, after all these years! But alas, it is not for me. I, for one, just want to see the looks on your faces; that will be reward enough. No, do not thank me, you will only embarrass me."

As he spoke, Antigone noticed that the view overhead was indeed shifting. From a clear moonlit sky, the view dissolved into a ghostlit wall of fog that was obviously no skyscape that could be glimpsed from New York City. And then again into a serene, leafy rainforest canopy.

"Stop it!" Antigone shouted. "Stop this right now. You win. Just tell us what you want from us so we can all get the hell out of here."

"What I want," Estevez said, "is not to have to think about the three of you anymore. I made you a generous offer and you threw it back in my face. But enough about my problems.

118 / Eric Griffin

Tomorrow, as they say, is another day. And I'm sure the sunrise will bring me fresh perspective. Yes, in the light of day, it may well be that all my worries will seem no more substantial than dust and ashes."

Antigone took his meaning only too clearly. "Eugenio, there must be something I can do to convince you to let at least Felton and Charlie go free. We'll bind them with blood promises. We'll erase their memories. We'll—"

"Like hell we will!" Felton interrupted, but Antigone did not dignify his outburst with anything more than an angry glance.

"No, no," Estevez said. "I have withdrawn my offer. Trust me. This is the best way, for all of us."

The scenery overhead continued to drift past. Antigone could see their time running out, flowing past them.

"Then there is nothing I can say or do to change your mind?" she demanded.

"I'm afraid I must agree with your assessment of the situation, Ms. Baines. It's a shame. I would have far preferred that we had not reached this particular impasse, but here we are. Out of time, out of options."

"Then you leave me no choice," she said.

"Precisely."

"What I mean is, you leave me no choice but to offer formal challenge. As prescribed by the rule of our order."

"I'm very sorry, Antigone, but there will be no further appeal. The decision rests with me. Regent Sturbridge, as you are doubtless aware, has been recalled to the Fatherhouse in Vienna. And that leaves me, temporarily of course, the ranking representative of the Pyramid in our fair city. I am sorry, Antigone, but I'm afraid I must reaffirm my earlier decision. You and your little cabal—your Conventicle, I believe you call it—are all under sentence of summary execution for your part in the conspiracy to assassinate the prince."

"No, you don't understand," Antigone said. "I am not challenging your decision, I am challenging you personally, according to the ancient rite as set down by our Father and Founder. I demand trial by *certámen*."

Estevez was dumbstruck. Then a smile creased his face. And before long, he was laughing aloud. "You?" he demanded. "You really must excuse me, novitia, but this is quite…" he broke down into a renewed fit of mirth. "Quite an *unexpected* turn of events."

Antigone glowered at the reflective glass. "As you say, I would have preferred that it not have come to this, but you have given me no other choice."

"Oh, I believe you, Ms. Baines, I quite believe that you are out of options. But the fact remains that you are now only stalling. You know perfectly well that you, a mere novice and not even—I trust you will forgive me for pointing it out—not even a particularly *gifted* novice… No, it is preposterous! Please do not get me wrong. While I am impressed that you managed to dig up some passing reference in your studies to the refined art of arcane combat, you must admit that your knowledge can only be of the most cursory and purely academic nature. I, on the other, hand, am an accomplished thaumaturge, and not unfamiliar with the form of combat you are attempting to invoke. No, it simply cannot be done. It would be a mere mockery of one of our most sacred rites to even consider such a challenge. And there certainly would be no honor in it. To slay a defenseless novice, one who has not mastered even the most basic of the blood arts! No, it is quite impossible. It was a noble attempt, I will give you that. But quite out of the question."

"I was not giving you a choice," Antigone said. "I was demanding trial by *certámen*. To be judged according to the most ancient tradition of our noble house."

"Then you are a very foolish young lady," Estevez said. "Very well then, issue your challenge. If you should best me in this ill-considered attempt, then you and your friends go free."

"That wasn't precisely what I had in mind," Antigone said. "I challenge you for your writ of *charter*. When I best you, you will yield your right to hear cases and sit in judgment *in loco regentiae*, during High Regent Sturbridge's absence."

"And then you will overturn your own case? Yes, I see. You are not without ambition. Very well, be it on your own head, then. As the challenged, it is my right to set three conditions on the contest. If you fail to abide by any of these conditions, you forfeit. Is that understood?"

Antigone vaguely remembered reading something along those lines before, but she could not say with certainty whether it was in the context of the established conventions of the *certámen*, or in some case of a protest over abuses of its ancient strictures. At this point, she felt she had little choice but to accede. She nodded for him to continue.

"My first condition is that of the location of the contest. It will take place in the grand foyer of the Chantry of Five Boroughs."

Antigone started to protest. The last thing she could afford to do was return to the chantry at this point. As things stood now, she was a fugitive from the Tremere Pyramid. She was under no illusions as to the fate that would await her within the chantry walls, at the hands of the astors if she should show her face there again. Still, it seemed it was a choice of that or a swift and fiery end for both herself and her companions.

"Done," she said. "Your second condition?"

"My second condition is that I place you under a strict oath of silence between now and the *certámen* proper. You shall not speak to anyone of me—that includes our meeting, our imminent challenge, and especially your groundless accusations against my person—until after the conclusion of our business. You understand? Good. Also, since I cannot rely upon your associates here to abide by the conventions of our people, they will remain here until after the challenge."

Again Antigone wanted to argue, but knew she was out of options. She cast a worried look at the unfamiliar sky through the window overhead, trying to gauge how many hours might be remaining before sunup. Without knowing even where that window looked out, it was hard to say. But it would be a few hours still. She hoped it would be enough.

"All right," she said. "That's two. Your last condition?"

"My final restriction will wait until just before the challenge. It will give you something to think on in the meanwhile. I will return to the chantry directly to prepare the rite. I suggest, for the sake of your friends that you do the same. Please convince your associates to step back and I will open the door for you. Temporarily, of course."

Antigone turned to Charlie and Felton. "I'm sorry," she said. "I tried. There was just no other—"

"Shh," Charlie interrupted. "Don't worry about us. You go take care of business. We'll be here. We're not going anywhere."

"Felton?" she asked hesitantly.

Felton contemplated his shoes.

Antigone tried to smile and scooped up her handbag off the vanity. She fumbled with the ritual trappings that still lay scattered on the counter. In the end, she gave up and just shoveled everything back into her bag, spilling chalk and melted wax on the floor.

"Well, then, I guess this is goodbye," she said. She shouldered her bag, straightened and started for the door. Felton stepped to block her way.

"If you think I'm just gonna let you—"

She cut him off, pressing a finger to his lips. "Goodbye, Mr. Felton."

He jerked away from her touch. "This has got to be about the worst idea you've ever had. Not that you haven't had some real winners before...."

"Wish me luck, Felton."

He recognized the look of determination on her face. She would not change her mind. Nor would he ever see her again. He shook his head and snorted. "Break a neck," he said.

She smiled and started past him, but he stopped her again, this time awkwardly putting his arms around her. "You give 'em one for me," he whispered.

Antigone returned the gesture briefly. She found herself staring stiffly over his shoulder into the mirror. Even from that angle, she could detect nothing suspicious in his motions or manner as she felt the weight of the gun slide into her bag.

He pushed her away to arm's length and held her there just a fraction of a second, "Hell, you give him six for me."

She nodded stiffly and disengaged herself. Without a further word or look over her shoulder, she marched straight forward into the glass pane. It flickered as she contacted its surface, and then she was gone.

Felton could have sworn in that moment, just before the two met, he saw all the lines of her body bend and stretch towards the glass, like a droplet of water craning upwards with its entire being towards your outstretched finger.

He counted off the seconds. One... two... three...

Still there was no report of the pistol. He didn't understand it.

And then, suddenly, he thought he did.

He cursed and folded himself down to the floor to await the coming of the sun.

Chapter Twenty-One
A Flaming Sword

Helena stormed through the empty corridors, head down, hands thrust deeply into the pockets of her robes. She did not slow until she heard the sound of her own footfalls, echoing back to her from the vast open spaces of the grand foyer just ahead. Then, checking the corridor in both directions to ensure that she was not observed, she steeled herself and stepped out into the vast hall.

The chamber was silent and empty except for the small abandoned figure at its center, chained between two pillars.

Anise was still now, slumped forward. The chains were the only thing keeping her upright at this point. Helena could see where the edges of the iron cuffs cut deeply into the novice's wrists. Angry red streaks stained her arms to the elbows before vanishing into the dark recesses of her sleeves. A light patter of droplets had managed to effect their escape and lay fallen all about her, forming a curious pattern, a sanguine mosaic on the floor. To all outward appearances, Anise was dead. Her eyes were glassy and stared fixedly at some obscure detail on the ground.

"Anise!" Helena whispered sharply, creeping closer. "Anise, it's me, Helena. I... I told you I would come back for you. Are you all right?"

The novice's head swung slightly to one side, but she did not look up.

Suppressing her unease, Helena stepped forward. She was all too aware that she was putting herself within easy reach of the deadly claws and fangs. Anise was hurt, badly hurt. Helena knew that if she did manage to coax any response from the novice, it would most likely be a violent one. The adept had ample evidence that Anise had already lost her struggle against the ravages of the Beast. The primal animal urge to kill and to feed already had the upper hand. If the slumbering creature chose this moment to awaken...

A tortured groan escaped cracked lips. At these close quarters, Helena could see that those lips were split and so very pallid. All the color had bled out of them. A pair of sightless white worms, curled in upon one another, each twisting to escape the light. There was a clink of chain and Helena saw one of the girl's hands tighten into a fist—its fingers entwining the crusted iron links. Helena knew she must work quickly now.

Raising her right hand to her mouth, Helena sliced into her thumb with the edge of an extended fang. She knotted her other fist into the novice's tangled mop of long red hair, jerking her head back so that she stared directly into Anise's eyes.

As soon as she made contact with the novice, the stern voice of the security daemon crackled from speakers around the room. "Security violation warning: Physical contact with the condemned is forbidden. Helena, Adepta, you will release the prisoner immediately and retreat three paces. Failure to comply will result in—"

"Override," Helena called, irritably. "Emergency medical intervention." Her voice was calm and steady. Her eyes bore into Anise's but there was no hint of recognition there—hardly any flicker of awareness at all.

With her bleeding thumb, Helena traced a four-pointed star on the novice's forehead.

"Access denied," replied the systems daemon. "Prisoner is condemned to death. Medical assistance is deemed in direct conflict to this sentence. Further efforts to render medical aid will be interpreted as an attempt to subvert just sentencing and will result in your acquisition as a target."

As the faint aroma of vitae washed over her, Anise's eyes flickered once, twice....

Helena slapped the novice across the face, hard enough to snap her head back.

"What the...?" Anise's disoriented mumble was nearly drowned beneath the hiss and whine of the defensive systems pivoting and targeting.

Helena quickly stepped backward, her hands dropping to her sides. Demonstrating to the security daemon that she posed no threat.

"Helena?" Anise asked. She took a hesitant step towards her superior and looked puzzled when she could advance no further. She stared uncomprehendingly at the taut length of chain that held her in place.

"Target acquired," the daemon said, louder this time. "Helena, Adepta, you have been instructed to retreat to a distance of three paces and hold that position. Further attempts to contact the condemned in any way—whether to help or to harm her—will be met with force."

Helena retreated another step. Her eyes bore into the novice's. She could see the struggle taking place there, as the Beast shrugged off its restless slumber and pawed towards the surface of her consciousness. There was very little time now and Helena had to make her understand.

"I am sorry, Anise," Helena said. "I told you I would come back for you, to get you out of this mess."

"I...I don't understand," the novice stammered. Then, desperately, "I didn't tell them! I didn't tell them anything. I don't know how they knew. They kept asking me the same questions, over and over again. About the fire, about the prisoner, about Antigone. But they wouldn't listen. What was I supposed to tell them?" She was nearly sobbing.

Helena shook her head. "It's all right. You did right. It's all over now. They can't hurt you anymore."

With her still-bleeding thumb, she traced the pattern of a four-pointed star upon her left hand. It stretched from the tip of her middle finger over the hump of her wrist and halfway down her forearm. It was Sturbridge's symbol. The flaming sword. The seal was worked into the very marble of the dais in the Hall of Audiences. Helena had stood upon it, just a short while before, when she had confronted Himes and Stephens and been humiliated.

If the regent were here, Helena thought, this is what *she* would have done.

Helena's left arm—palm down and fully extended straight from the shoulder—cut a swift arc between them in the air. It passed within a handbreadth of the novice's throat, never touching her. As it did so, light flared from the star upon Anise's brow and that upon Helena's palm.

Anise's head fell back and tumbled from her shoulders, cleanly severed.

Helena had kept her promise. She had returned for the novice and freed her, carrying her forever beyond the reach of the astors.

Helena, however, had little time to enjoy her defiance. There was a loud retort and the sizzling smell of ozone, and Helena slumped insensate to the marble floor.

Chapter Twenty-Two
Mascara Tears

A ntigone slowed coming into sight of the gutted ruin that had, until recently, been Franklin #3 High School. She had not been back here since the night of the fire, the night that she and Johanus had barely escaped the building before it blew.

The sight of it now, its immediacy, brought her up short. The facade of the building was smudged black, streaked as if by mascara tears. It dabbed at the shattered windows of its eyes with large squares of plywood. The roof had given way entirely in places and even now a tentative wisp of smoke wound skywards from the rubble.

It was almost too much to take in. That night, the commandeered gymnasium had been packed with Kindred — refugees fleeing the ravages of the Sabbat's brutal conquest of the eastern seaboard. Antigone tried to calculate the loss. The casualties of this single night's terror probably exceeded the entire vampiric population of many Camarilla cities. They had come in droves to present themselves before the prince, as required by Tradition. To ask his blessing before setting up shop in the recently liberated Camarilla city—the last remaining stronghold on the East Coast against the advance of the ravening Sabbat.

These were the people of the aftermath, a flood tide of outcasts and immigrants, opportunists and prospectors, pariahs, carpetbaggers, anarchs, pioneers and outlaws that had washed over the city. Each of the newcomers had been intent on carving out his own piece of the blood-red Big Apple. It seemed everyone had a dream, or at least a scheme. But in a moment, all their plans, hopes, ambitions, aspirations had been swept away in a holocaust of flame.

She had run out on Johanus that night, abandoned him to the herculean cleanup job. The task of removing all evidence that anything unusual had been taking place here—and of smoothing things over with local police, fire, rescue and press crews—was certainly not one she envied him. Nor would he be likely to quickly forgive her for ducking out on him.

But she had to try. She didn't have anyone else to turn to. Antigone had been cast out and declared a renegade by her own house. And now she was returning to the chantry to face the wrath of Estevez and the astors. The special operatives from Vienna had a reputation for the ruthless efficiency with which they dealt with problems. And they certainly had no reason to remember Antigone fondly.

She could go back to the Nosferatu. Emmett had reluctantly agreed to help her and keep her safe, in accordance with Sturbridge's parting request. And he had done so. Antigone, however, did not know how long she could rely on his continued good graces.

And Emmett was the wrong one to call on for help in this situation. He had a personal grudge to settle with Mr. Felton and all of Antigone's carefully marshaled arguments had not been able to convince the bull-headed Nosferatu otherwise.

So, here she was. Johanus had the knowledge and the thaumaturgic expertise to help get Felton and Charlie out of their current predicament. Plus he had always been kind to her in the past. Antigone did not delude herself that this was because of any particular affection he had for her. But Johanus had been one of the better masters of novices during Antigone's protracted apprenticeship, and his protective attitude toward his charges still colored their relationship.

Antigone had never abused his trust and, even after Johanus had been assigned to other duties—under circumstances which had caused something of a scandal at the time—she had always made a point of treating him just the same, as a confidante and a mentor. Thus it was no coincidence that he, in return, still looked upon Antigone as someone to be protected, instructed and set back on the correct path when she strayed. Antigone knew that the adept's first instinct would be to help her, if he could do so. She was counting on getting what she needed before his better judgment kicked in.

The main doors to the school had been knocked in with a fire ax. A chain-link enclosure, topped with barbed wire, now barred the entrance in an attempt to keep anyone from wandering into the condemned building. The gate was padlocked, but this proved little obstacle to Antigone. She took the lock in one hand and twisted. It snapped, accompanied by the high metallic note of a spring bouncing away across the concrete. She closed the gate behind her and tossed the remains of the padlock onto the cracked pavement.

The lights were out inside the school, which was a small blessing. Almost immediately Antigone stumbled over some unidentified mass in the darkness that squelched underfoot. She tried not to think about what it might once have been and pressed on down the hall. She trailed a hand along one wall and it came away covered with a thick blackened sludge. Making her way more by memory than by sight, she reached the gymnasium.

The swinging doors had been knocked from their hinges and lay face down, jutting from beneath the pile of rubble, just inside the opening. The entire room was lit with a ghostly illumination. Each rough edge of splintered wood, each shard of broken masonry was highlighted by the faint azure glow. It didn't take long for Antigone to determine the source of this phenomenon—moonlight diffusing through the blue tarp that had been thrown over the gaping hole in the roof.

Antigone stepped gingerly over the threshold, groping for the nearest wall and balance. The filtered moonlight gave her skin an unhealthy blue undertone. She was struck by her resemblance to a drowned corpse. It was not a flattering comparison. She found herself thinking of her recent sojourn among the dead, of the jackal god's pool of suicides, of the nightmare of the Children Down the Well.

The deserted gymnasium cut quite a contrast to her memory of it from her previous visit. She tried to recall the details of that night, if nothing else, to banish the other unsettling images racing through her thoughts. On that occasion—had it been just a week before?—the thing that stuck out in her mind was the claustrophobic press of bodies. She couldn't recall with certainty what colors the gym had been painted, or even being able to see the walls for the throng.

The vast hall was empty now, quiet. She realized coming here had been a mistake. The life—or that spark of inhuman hunger that fed upon life—had gone out of the place. She picked her way across the rubble to the far door. She would check the basement before giving the effort up for lost. That had been Johanus's command center. If he were here, that is where the work would be tonight.

She swung through the double doors, the first set she had found still standing, and struck off down the corridor until she came to a door labeled *Boiler Room. Maintenance Personnel Only.* She put one hand to the knob to force the door, but found that the knob turned freely in her grasp. Cautiously, she descended the metal stairway into the cellar.

She doubted that the ravages of the fire would have spread this far. There was no sign of scorching on the wooden door upstairs, and fires are creatures of habit—generally burning upward, not down. Unless given a pretty good reason to go against their natural inclinations.

Of course, the tons of falling masonry overhead may well have caused the ceiling here to collapse or the foundation to shift, so it was still a good idea to be careful.

The fact that there was a dim light shining up at her from the darkness below also spoke of the need for caution.

Chapter Twenty-Three
The Infirmary

Sturbridge slowly drifted back towards consciousness. She seemed to be floating face down, one hand trailing out to her side. Someone was holding firmly to that hand.

She tried to roll over, but the sharp tearing pain in the back of her leg stopped her. The medium she floated upon, she realized, was not water, but wool. Thick, undyed woolen blankets wrapped tightly above and below. Beneath the blankets, her skin was damp with blood-sweat—the last telltale sign of the broken fever.

Very slowly she turned her head and saw Dorfman scowling down at her from her bedside.

"So you're back among us at last." He absently patted Sturbridge's hand, then, with some embarrassment, relinquished it altogether. "I was beginning to fear there would be no one to keep me company on the chopping block."

Sturbridge tried a smile but the attempt came out more of a grimace. "Then the councilor, she knows…"

"Hush. Save your strength. The doctor says you need rest. But you've been tossing all night. Ah, good. Here he is now."

Dorfman raised his voice, and called loudly, perhaps too loudly for the confines of the tiny room, "Herr Doktor?"

Doktor Lohm scowled, stooped over Sturbridge and put the back of a wrinkled, spotted hand to her forehead. Sturbridge could feel each bone of that hand.

"She should be resting," he said disapprovingly. "The fever's broken. Let me see that leg. No, hold still."

Sturbridge could not see what he was doing from her angle. She opted to bear it with as much dignity as she could muster under the circumstances. She heard the rustle of blankets, but otherwise would not have known that the fabric had been pulled aside. She didn't feel much of anything below her right knee.

The doctor slowly peeled back the linen bandages and Dorfman let out a low whistle, seeing the swollen and blackened calf where the blood serpent had struck her. Doktor Lohm shot him a disapproving glance.

"You're a very lucky young woman, Miss Sturbridge," Lohm said. "A very lucky young woman. You will need more salve, new bandages, and I have prepared for you a draught for the pain. Peter will, no doubt, help you with these. Given that he flatly refuses to leave, he might at least make himself useful."

"How long?" Sturbridge managed to force the words past her parched throat. "How long have I been…"

If the doctor heard her question, he made no response. "You will need blood. I will send to the cellars for someone bland and docile. You should be able to manage that, even in your present condition. See if you can't get her to drink something, Peter. Just a little." He straightened up and turned to leave.

"Thank you, Herr Doktor," Sturbridge said, her voice sounding clearer this time, stronger.

"It is nothing, Miss Sturbridge. My master, he remembers you well from your last visit to us. We are all very sorry that this has happened." He turned to Dorfman. "I can only hope," he said pointedly, "that your business here has been brought to its conclusion. I cannot stress how important it is that the regent return to somewhere quiet for her convalescence."

"Thank you, Herr Doktor," Dorfman said. "How long do you think it will be? Before she can travel, I mean."

"To my mind," he said, "the dangers of relocating the patient are minimal—a possible aggravation of the wound. While the risk of remaining here... well, let us say that the regent will make a speedier recovery surrounded by her own people, her own things."

He started to say something more, then caught himself and turned towards the door. "Rest now," he called back over his shoulder. "The worst has passed. I see no reason why you shouldn't be up and around by this time tomorrow night."

The door shut quietly behind him.

Dorfman busied himself with arranging bandages. He wouldn't meet Sturbridge's eyes.

After an uncomfortable pause, Sturbridge broke the silence. "Well, it can't be that bad."

"No, you're going to be fine, fine. Didn't the doctor say so? There's little profit in lying to those near death. It's like taking your boat out in a thunderstorm—the heavens are hanging just a bit too low for you to be drawing such attention down upon yourself."

"Well, then, what's wrong?"

"It's nothing. Sorry. I didn't mean to say, you know, 'near death.' You're going to be fine, really. It's just..."

"It's just what?" Sturbridge was growing impatient.

"I should have seen it coming, is all. I'm sorry. I should never have brought you here in the first place."

"It's not your fault," Sturbridge replied.

"Try telling that to the councilor. The situation is just too tenuous right now. We're getting you out of here. Tonight."

Chapter Twenty-Four
Sciencia's Subterranean Lair

The flickering red light below spoke of an open flame somewhere just ahead. It made Antigone reconsider her earlier conclusions about the fire not having reached this level. She stopped, still four or five steps from the bottom.

"Johanus?" she called. "Umberto? Is anyone here?"

Her only answer was the crackle and pop of burning wood. The smell that billowed up to her, however, was the reek of melting plastic.

She could see now that the light streamed outward through the grate of the ancient boiler. Not the one that had until recently heated the school, but the old cast-iron dinosaur that slumped against one wall of the cellar. Its rusty grate stood ajar, the metal glowing red-hot from the blaze stoked within.

Antigone was distracted by a long shadow breaking loose from its fellows and sweeping like a searchlight across the cellar floor.

"You should not have come," said a solemn voice. There was a metallic squeal and a rustle of papers, and the light from below flared up. It cast upon the room an infernal luminance and revealed the figure crouched at the maw of the cast-iron beast.

He was broad shouldered, but stooped. The firelight set his red beard glowing like a coat of mail being forged. His features were blunt and weathered from a life that had been lived outdoors and in direct contest with the elements. A powerful frame spoke, not of a life of toil, but of physical rigors of a self-inflicted variety—of mountains scaled, of polar vistas crossed and conquered. In another time, he might been a figure stepping from the rolling deck of a Viking longship.

Now there was a weariness about him, a forced stillness that he wore like an ill-fitting suit. Barely contained anger peeked out of him, like glimpses of wrist that too-short shirtsleeves refused to cover.

"Johanus," she said. "I'm glad I found you here. I didn't know where else to look."

"You can thank Umberto. He picked you up on the security camera when you busted in the front gate. That was really stupid, by the way. He said he thought I might want to get over here before someone else got to you first."

"I'm sorry. I wouldn't have come if there was any other way. I… I need your help."

Johanus snorted. "It seems I've helped you too much already."

Not exactly the reaction she'd counted on. Something must have happened. But what?

"What's that supposed to mean?"

"Come on, Antigone. You know I can't help you now. After what you've done, I…" He broke off and swore. "I shouldn't have helped you the last time you came here. And I wouldn't have if I'd known."

"You mean about the bombing?"

"I mean about the astors." He turned upon her, rising to his full height.

"Oh," she said quietly. The simple admission had the effect she intended. Johanus had been prepared for denials, arguments, excuses. Her answer seemed to cut the legs out from under his rising anger. He snorted and turned away from her.

"Did you think I wouldn't know?" he said. "That I wouldn't find out? Jeez, you think you can just waltz right back in here and pull the same stunt all over again. You are a fugitive, Antigone. A renegade. You know what they told me to do if I should see you again?"

Antigone descended the last few steps and walked straight up to him. She stuck out her chin defiantly, which came about as high as his sternum, and raised one finger threateningly. She knew she posed about as much of a physical threat to him as she did to the mammoth cast-iron boiler. "Bring her in," she said. "Dead or alive!"

"Stop fooling around, Antigone. This isn't funny." He gently pushed her away, shaking his head. "What the hell am I supposed to do with you?"

"I take it that means you're not turning me in for the reward," she said.

"I told you, that's not funny."

"So what did they do, lean on you a little bit? Maybe rough you up?"

"You just don't care do you?" he demanded. "About the mess you've made of things. About all the trouble you've caused. About who gets hurt. As long as you get to walk away from it all."

Antigone shook her head. "It's not like that. You know it's not. I'm one of the victims here, remember? I'm the one on the receiving end of the astors' witch-hunt. Look, I know I've made a mess of things recently, but I'm going to make things right. And I need your help."

"I can't do that." Johanus turned away from her and crouched over the pile of debris stacked in front of the old boiler. He scooped up a stack of computer printouts and a tangle of cabling and shoved them through the grate.

"Look, it's not like I'm asking you to go up against the astors or anything. I just need you to help a couple of friends out of a jam."

Johanus stood and fished a set of car keys out of his pocket and held them out to her. "Here. It's parked out back, an old Dodge Ram. You can't miss it. It's not much to look at, but it will get you the hell away from here. You need to get out of town."

"I can't do that," she countered. "I made a promise."

"Antigone, I..." He took her hand and opened his mouth to say something, then stopped. "I'm sorry, Antigone." He closed her fingers around the car keys and let go of her hand.

"So that's it?" she demanded. "You're not even going to hear me out? I only came here tonight because I thought I could count on you. I'm sorry I even bothered." She hurled the keys towards the grate, but they rebounded with a clatter off the side of the boiler.

He spun at the sound, but checked himself and let the keys lie where they had fallen.

"I know you won't understand," he muttered, "but there really is nothing I can do to help you. And if the astors ever find out that I let you walk out of here, it's as much as my miserable hide is worth. You've already got enough deaths to answer for; I don't intend to be number three."

Antigone started to protest her innocence, to explain that the deaths of the three novices in the burning *domicilium* had been unavoidable. That she had been in the right. She had been faced with an impossible dilemma, but had tackled it head-on and saved the chantry in the process. She knew these arguments and counterarguments by heart. She had run through them, self-accused, a hundred times. Every time she closed her eyes, it seemed.

Then his words sank in. He didn't intend to be death number *three*? For a moment a surge of pure hope and elation shot through her. Had there been some mistake? Had one of the novices actually managed to get out of that inferno? It didn't seem possible. It seemed too much to hope for.

Then another possibility occurred to her and she felt a sudden weight of dread settle into the pit of her stomach.

"What do you mean about not wanting to be death number three?" she asked, already dreading the answer. "Three novices died in that fire in the *domicilium*. That would make you the fourth death they have laid at my doorstep."

Johanus looked irritated. "I'm not talking about the damned fire. I'm talking about—" He broke off.

There was an uncomfortable silence and then he said. "You don't know. Of course you don't. How could you? Did you think that there wouldn't be any repercussions to your little stunt that night? You lied to me, Antigone. And then you ran out and left me to deal with the aftermath of the explosion here by myself. That much I know. The rest is only hearsay. They tell me that you broke into the chantry. That you disabled the defensive network and then freed a bunch of prisoners and then started another fire to cover your escape."

He glared at her, daring her to deny the charges. Again her first reaction was to protest, but she thought better of it. "I couldn't just let them kill Felton," she said instead. "Or to turn him over to the prince's men or the police—which would have amounted to the same thing."

"I hope it was worth it. If it wasn't for your little stunt that night," Johanus said, "Helena and Anise would still be with us."

Antigone felt the ground wheel under her. Helena? Anise? Destroyed? She heard each of his words but none of them found any purchase upon her understanding. It just couldn't be. Monstrously, Johanus kept on speaking as if unaware of the impossibility of his words or the effect they produced upon her. Antigone could only catch the tail end of what he said.

"We've all suffered enough already, Antigone. It would be best if you were to just go."

"I don't understand," she said. "How did this happen?"

"Didn't you once stop to think, only for a moment, that there would be repercussions? Didn't you care who would be left to take the blame?"

"Helena was fine when I left her that night. She said she'd square everything."

"So that's it?" he demanded. "You just washed your hands of the whole affair? Well, let me tell you about what came of your ill-considered jailbreak. Anise was the security officer on duty that night. What do think the astors would have done to you if it had been on your watch? Someone breaks into the chantry, sabotages the security-system grid, frees a prisoner, attacks a novice, sets fire to the novice *domicilium*. How did you think the astors were going to take that?"

"Jeez, Anise was on duty? But it wasn't her fault. As soon as the security daemon shut down and went into diagnostic mode she would have had her hands too full to worry about much else. Helena could have told them—" Antigone broke off.

"Helena was in no position to 'tell' anybody anything. Not surprisingly, she immediately found herself on the receiving end of all the telling. The astors needed someone to make an example of, and Anise fit the bill."

Feelings of frustration, resentment and utter powerlessness, chased one other through Antigone's stomach. "What did they do?" Her voice was a dangerous rumble through clenched teeth.

"They ordered that she be stoned. Once in torpor, she was to be put to Final Death. Staked for the dawn or some such."

An animal wail of rage and denial broke from Antigone's throat. Johanus, however, now having embarked on his monstrous litany of events, could not stop. He had to tell the whole of it. There was no other way to free himself, if only for a short time, of the heinous images.

"They dragged her, in chains, to the grand foyer and hung her there between two pillars. They took a pile of debris, broken stone and concrete, from the ruins of the novice *domicilium* and stacked it before her. Then they herded all the other novices before her and compelled them to cast stones."

Antigone shook her head vehemently. "No. No, that can't be. They wouldn't have done it. They would have refused. They..."

"The novices understood the situation. To refuse was more than simply to invite unwelcome suspicions—it was to disobey a direct order from the Fatherhouse. Some obeyed only half-heartedly, but they obeyed."

Antigone's face was in her hands, as if by this means she could block out the horrible images, the cruel stones that Johanus cast at her. Still, the words would not stop.

"She proved very resilient," Johanus's voice droned on, maddeningly calm. "I have never witnessed a stoning. It is my understanding that among mortals, these barbarities come to a swift and sure end within a matter of minutes. After the first hour, there was little trace of the human left about Anise. She was bleeding from dozens of wounds—reduced to little more than a howling animal, cornered and dying."

"Stop it," Antigone muttered angrily. She struck out at him blindly. Memories of the long nights that she had spent training the hesitant young security-team recruit kept leaping out to ambush her. When Anise had first come to them, her concept of a computer was something that took up an entire basement and operated by means of some obscure Tarot-like divination involving the reading of punch cards. It was not her fault, Antigone had kept reminding herself. Anise was—like all of them—a product of her times. A time when a proper young lady did not stoop to frequent the rumbling, late-night, subterranean lair of *sciencia*.

But Anise had been a quick study and she was certainly one of the best security officers.... Antigone could not complete the thought. Could not reconcile it to the monstrous reality that Johanus recounted. The story was fantastical. It could not be true. Only the absolutely calm, emotionless voice with which he told it brought the truth of the matter home to her. Anise was no longer one of the chantry's best security officers. She was no longer anything but a rapidly decomposing corpse.

Mercifully, Johanus had fallen silent at last. He had suffered stoically her efforts to push him away, to strike him. They were, so far as he was concerned, inconsequential. To Antigone, however, the blows struck true; they stemmed the damning litany.

"You asked me what happened," Johanus said. "So I'm telling you what happened. If you don't want to hear it, fine. Nobody's keeping you here. Get out. I've got other things to do anyway." He returned to feeding rubbish into the fire.

Antigone struggled for control. At last she managed. "You said both Anise and Helena were... What happened to Helena?"

"What the hell do you care?"

"Damn it, Johanus! I lived and worked side by side with her for the better part of seventy years. I think I've got the right to know what happened to her at least."

"You don't have any rights, period. You're a renegade, remember? And if you cared so damned much about what happened to her, you wouldn't have set her up like that."

"What? I didn't set anyone up. Helena didn't do anything different than you just did, giving me those truck keys and telling me to get out of town. Helena told me I needed to get out of the chantry fast and she said she'd square things up. And I believed her. If Helena said she'd cover my back, I knew she'd cover my back. I did what she told me; I got out. She didn't say anything about anyone getting killed!"

"Well, you should have known," said Johanus grumpily. "You can't screw around with the astors and expect that everything will just somehow work itself out."

"I'm sorry," Antigone said. "Do you really think that if I knew that they would take this all out on Helena that I would have just left her there? Hell, I would have made her come with me. Somehow," she finished, less confidently.

Johanus cursed. "She knew all this would come down on her. She had known for months, ever since Foley was assassinated. She told me as much. She must have thought if she just played along with them, if she gave them what they wanted—delivered up the regent, handed over the security codes and signed over a chantry full of well-behaved pretty young novices all in a row—that that would be enough. But she didn't count on you. You just kept screwing things up."

Antigone felt the accusation strike home, but she mustered up what courage remained to her. "Johanus, what happened to Helena?"

"I should take you back there," he mused aloud without turning from the flames. "That way you could see her for yourself. With your own eyes. After all, you have a *right* to."

Antigone felt distinctly uncomfortable with this turn in the conversation. "Johanus, please. I've got to know. How can I leave here without knowing what happened to Helena?"

"They left her there," he said, his voice cracking with indignation. "I've never seen anything like it. They hung her up, suspended at the very crux—between life and death. Like some damned trophy. They tell me the novices won't even walk past the grand foyer anymore. Yes, they made a point of telling me that. They were proud of the fact, the bastards. Guess they got that 'example' they wanted."

Chapter Twenty-Five
A Miscarried Insinuation

"I take it that you are, erhm, quite satisfied then, Mr. Stephens?" Himes followed his fellow astor into the regent's sanctum. He barely avoided being caught as the reinforced steel door clanged shut at his heels with the angry hiss of hydraulic bolts shooting into place. Himes took off his spectacles and polished the lenses with a handkerchief.

Stephens was used to his partner's perambulations by now. He knew there was something bothering Himes. Stephens even had a pretty good idea what it was.

"Why shouldn't I be satisfied?" he said, crossing the room to the computer terminal and thumbing it to life. "Our work here is nearly done. The chantry is secured. We have restored a proper sense of fear and obedience among the novitiate. The guilty parties have been ferreted out and punished. What's not to be satisfied about?"

He cast about for a chair so that he might sit down at the terminal. All of the major furnishing—the cast-iron canopy bed, the desk, the tumbledown throne of books—had been removed from the sanctum. Sturbridge's remaining possessions had been crated, coded, and stacked neatly along one wall. One of these crates had already been commandeered for a monitor stand. Stephens crossed the room to retrieve another to use as a makeshift chair.

Himes cleared his throat, in prelude to some reproach, no doubt. Stephens hastened to cut him off.

"Okay, I know we're a bit behind schedule. But with all the unanticipated complications we've run into here onsite—not to mention all the commotion this operation has kicked up back at the Fatherhouse—surely Dorfman won't begrudge us a little time to make sure this is done and done right. The last thing any of us wants is to have to send a team back in here again. What's a few more nights to him, after all? He's hoarded up thousands of them; he can spare a couple."

Himes frowned down at his lenses disapprovingly, then returned them to his face. "Lord Dorfman tends to be rather punctilious. And the fact is, the work here is not quite completed yet."

Stephens waved dismissively. He wasn't about to let Himes shake his good mood. "Nothing left but the washing-up," he said. "A few more security-team members to stake out for the sunrise, all just routine stuff. I don't even think there'll be much resistance at this point. The fight's gone out of them. Once they saw what happened to Sturbridge and Anise—and to Helena! Now *that* is how you make a point, Himes. Well, let's just say the worst is behind us now."

He bent over the crate, took hold of it and straightened, but only with apparent effort. "Jeez, what the hell did you guys pack in these crates? This one weighs about a—" He broke off, seeing, out of the corner of his eye, Himes fidget uncomfortably from one foot to another. He set the crate down heavily.

"A few souvenirs, perhaps?" Stephens pressed. "A little something to be retrieved quietly once we returned to Vienna? It seems to me that, with all the boxes so carefully labeled, it would be simplicity itself to find the correct crate again. Even if it were stored among hundreds of others just like it."

Himes rolled his eyes. "Simplicity itself. They are books, Mr. Stephens. Sturbridge's books. You will recall that our orders specify that all of the regent's possessions were to be transported back to the Fatherhouse."

"Oh, I see. Books. You can tell that by these numerals here I take it?" Stephens walked the length of the wall of crates. At the end, he found one, only half-full, that had been left open to receive any last minute odds and ends. He also found what he was looking for.

Returning with the hammer, he wedged its claw under the lip of his makeshift chair. "Anything else in this one, judging by the markings of course?" he asked with a predatory smile. There was a sharp crack as the board gave way.

"Well, now that you mention it," Himes muttered, "there is also a curious artifact we came across, nothing that would interest you, of course...."

Stephens began rooting through the contents of the crate, tossing books and manuscripts—many of which were, no doubt, irreplaceable—to the floor.

"At present, our experts' best guess," Himes called over the racket, "is that the device may allow its user—under the proper astrological alignments, you understand—to make a complete ass of himself."

Stephens, surrounded now by a cairn of heaped tomes, stopped. He glanced at the volume in his hand as if failing to recognize what it was or how he might have come by it, and let it fall disdainfully back into the nearly empty crate. He heard it hit the wood of the crate bottom.

"May I ask," he said, his voice icy and formal, "why you are in such a foul mood tonight? If I didn't know better, I'd think it had something to do with that traitor, Helena. You've been out of sorts ever since we carried out her sentence this evening. Surely you hadn't developed a fondness for her. No, no. I am willing to admit that there was much to admire about her—the casual manner in which she sold out her regent, for example.

Honestly, Himes, sometimes I think you have grown *sentimental* in your old age."

"Sentimental?" Himes said. He turned the word over, looking for some hidden or obscure meaning, but couldn't seem to make it fit. "I think, my friend, that you mistake me. No, it is not some attachment to the good adept that is responsible for my preoccupation this evening—for surely that is what you have sensed. It is rather that I am curious about your departure from our standard procedure in the matter of Helena's sentence. Had we not worked together for some decades already, I would suspect that there was some note of personal grudge or even vendetta to your actions. That is to say, if I hadn't known you to be such a consummate professional in all things."

Stephens looked up distractedly from his efforts to drag the half-emptied crate across the room. It bumped to a halt. "It wasn't too…" he paused, looking for a word, "showy, you don't think? It was a rather forceful statement and I do worry sometimes. The novices are so impressionable right now—after all that has happened—and it is crucial that we make precisely the right impression."

"That was rather along the same lines as what has been bothering me," Himes said. "I much prefer the usual—that is to say, mundane—methods. Maybe I am sentimental. Give me a good, old-fashioned stoning or staking or, in less severe cases, a stern dismemberment, just to give them something to think about for a while. But the use of the thaumaturgic arts? I must admit that this method leaves me a bit apprehensive. Even in a just punishment, such radical solutions are always going to be viewed as a bit extreme. And things could escalate. If the novices begin to feel threatened by our presence here, they might even attempt to reply in kind."

"Nonsense," Stephens said. "The very thought of a green novice attempting some kind of magical retaliation against—"

He broke off uncomfortably, recalling his all-too-recent encounter on the Widow's Walk. He turned angrily back towards his efforts with the crate. "All right, point taken. But we had to make a statement here. Obviously, the stonings and stakings just weren't getting through to them."

"I understand your concern," Himes said in a soothing tone. "And I publicly supported you in front of the novices, of course. It is such a little thing, you see, I even hesitated to place it before you privately. But since you broached the topic…"

"Yeah, well, you've said your piece; now I'm unbroaching it."

"Of course," Himes replied. "It was not my intention to make you uncomfortable."

"I'm not uncomfortable!" Stephens, having gotten the chair into position, sat down abruptly. "We did the right thing, okay?"

"You are, no doubt, correct. I should not have brought it up."

Stephens turned in his seat to face him. "Look, this place was a mess when we got here. A real mess. Novices dying in halls, visiting dignitaries murdered, official chantry communications doctored, and the regent gone clean off her rocker. A couple of the novices, the good ones, managed to come through all this. Nothing either of us is going to do at this point is going to hurt them any worse or push them over the edge. All right? We've done our job and we've done it well. Nobody has any grounds to reproach us."

"I am only glad it's over at last," Himes replied, bending over the pile of scattered tomes and beginning to restack them. "It's just that…"

"Just that what?" Stephens snapped.

"Just that, up until tonight, we had managed to run this investigation precisely…" he paused, a mangled volume in hand, "by the book. But that rite you invoked tonight…"

"You *do* think it was too showy," Stephens accused. "I do wish you'd just come right out and say what you mean sometimes. Look, these novices are alone and frightened. They've been abandoned by their regent. All they have left is the vague promise of a distant and benevolent Tremere authority that they've never seen. That's where we come in. When we're on the ground, we are the symbol of that authority. So when I see a threat—any threat—to this community, you had better believe I say something. And that I act swiftly and decisively. To do otherwise would be to betray the trust that has been placed in us."

"Yes, yes, noble words. I quite agree," Himes interrupted, shaking his head to free himself of the almost-hypnotic intensity in his partner's voice. "But it is this *particular* sentence that is bothering me. And I would request that in future, when you should feel called upon to make a—how did you put it?—swift and decisive decision that involves the use of thaumaturgy against our own charges, that you would do me the courtesy of first consulting with me."

"Oh, so *that's* what this is all about," Stephens said, smiling. "You're upset because you would have done something differently and didn't get a say in this matter."

"Nothing of the kind. I am concerned that you went to such lengths to assure that the body would be 'preserved.' To tell the truth I find your method distasteful. What exactly is that rite you employed? For, to tell you truly, it seemed to have as much in common with certain verboten diagrams as with any rites sanctioned by our elders."

"Ah, now we come to the crux of the matter," Stephens said. "I assure you that the diagram in question is quite legitimate. It is a variation on the protective circle of stasis first developed by Meerlinda herself back in the early sixteenth century. It—"

"I must confess, that comes as a relief. Any rite pioneered by the councilor herself must be the very height of orthodoxy. I will look into this matter further upon our next stopover at the Fatherhouse. You must forgive me my ungrounded suspicion. It was unworthy of me."

Himes' apology, and his mention of pursuing the matter further, didn't put Stephens any more at ease.

Chapter Twenty-Six
A Corpse, Nothing More

"So that's it," Antigone demanded. "The astors have condemned two of our sisters to death and you're just going to sit there?"

"There's nothing you can do for them now, Antigone."

"The hell there's not. From what you say they've got Helena strung up like some macabre trophy and have forbidden anyone to so much as approach the body. Helena deserves a decent burial at least. To be allowed to rest."

"You can't change the sentence of the astors," he said. "You try and you're only inviting a similar fate down upon yourself."

"You're telling me that you've seen her, with your own eyes, and yet you've done nothing?" She was incredulous. "I know you better than that, Johanus. You cannot possibly submit to such a desecration."

"She is a corpse, Antigone. Nothing more. Nothing worth losing your life over at this point. If only I had been there when they took her..."

"Oh yes, *then* you would have fought to save her from this. But now you won't raise a finger to help her?"

"Antigone, what can I do at this point? Nothing I could do would help Helena one bit. And I would pay for that empty defiance with my existence. No, I have sacrificed too much already to get where I am. I will remain the good and obedient servant of Clan Tremere." His voice dripped the acid of self-reproach.

"That does not sound like the adept I know. Tell me, then, if you won't do the deed yourself, if you will at least take up a share of the task."

"What *task* are you talking about? Oh, no. You can't possibly be thinking of..."

"I asked you earlier if you would help me for my own sake and you refused. I ask you again, will you help me for Helena's sake?"

"I don't believe this. Haven't you been listening to a word I've been saying? Helena is gone. Forget her. There's nothing you can do. By going back to the chantry now, you're only going to get more people killed. I... I can't let you do that, Antigone."

"I'll do my part—as well as yours—if you refuse me, *brother*." She spat the last word like an invective. "It's fine for you to sit back and accuse me of killing her, and I cannot refute your claims. But at least no one will ever be able to say that I betrayed her."

"I'm not going to sit here and listen to crap like that," he said. "I never betrayed Helena and you know it. Now you'd better just get out of here. You're talking nonsense and I've got better things to do than... Just go on." He scooped up the truck keys off the floor and tossed them to her. She caught them reflexively.

"You can't even say for sure if she is truly destroyed," she accused. "And what exactly would you call it when someone left his sister alone to die? Where I come from, that's betrayal. And so what if she is already dead? That's not an argument. You can't just leave her body to hang there, unmourned and desecrated. That's another betrayal. I don't know about you, but I intend to—"

"Careful," he warned. "It's one thing to be bold and outraged here, in private. You have had a nasty surprise and you are not yourself. But do not bind yourself to a course of action that you, upon more sober reflection, will find yourself unequal to. These astors, if they could do something like that to Helena—who was the best of us—will not be greatly taxed to do the same or worse to you."

"They've got no right!" Antigone raged at him. "They've got no right to keep her from us. She is our sister, one of our own. She deserves better. She will have better."

"I want you to think for a minute," Johanus said. "Think about this 'one of our own' business. Helena is beyond help, Antigone. Anise is dead. Sturbridge is gone—"

"Sturbridge is what?!" Estevez had said something like that about Sturbridge as well, but it hadn't really registered on Antigone at the time.

"Gone. Recalled to Vienna. To answer for all that has happened here. Surely you knew that was coming. It was inevitable."

Antigone *had* known it was coming. Sturbridge herself had said as much, that last night, on the widow's walk. "By tomorrow night, they may well have closed down the entire chantry," she had said. "But that still leaves us tonight to set right what we can."

Against her will, Antigone felt the first hint of blood welling up in the corners of her eyes. It was just too much. Sturbridge, Helena, Anise, all gone. Victims of the astors and their damned purge. *How many more,* she wondered, *will be sacrificed upon the altar of clan unity? Why did any of this have to happen? Why couldn't they just have left us alone?*

She realized Johanus was speaking, but now the very sound of his voice irritated her. "It will be over soon, now," he was saying. "With Helena out of their way, it's really just a matter of a few more 'routine executions' and the appointing of a new junior regent to help ease the transition to the new regime."

"Shut up!" she barked. She was trying to think and his matter-of-fact analysis of the monstrous reality was maddening. "That doesn't change anything. We've still got to do what is right. Even if it's too late to help Sturbridge or Anise, we can at least help Helena. And if we find that she's truly and finally dead, we can take down her remains, give her back some shred of dignity. That much, at least, we can do."

Johanus shook his head. "Think, Antigone. You and I, we are the remnant. We might well be the last two left of what you think of as our little brotherhood. Sturbridge, Helena, Anise, all of them have come to a tragic end. Think how much more miserably and unmourned we will die by defying the astors. We can't beat them; the entire power of the Pyramid stands behind them. The best we can do is put them to some trouble in having to invent a suitably grisly end to make a proper example of us."

Antigone angrily waved these concerns aside. "How can you just... no, never mind. I can see this isn't going to get us anywhere. Look, you just do what you have to do. And I'll do what I have to."

"Antigone, I can't let you do this. Think about what you're saying. Helena wouldn't want you to throw your life away for nothing. She wouldn't defy the astors and sacrifice everything just to get your rotting carcass back. She wouldn't ask you to do so for her."

"That doesn't matter," Antigone said. "She was my sister, more than a sister to me. Of all people I would think that you would appreciate that."

"Antigone..."

"If she has survived this far, I'll get her out of there. If she is fully dead, I'll bury her. She deserves at least that much."

"And what if the astors aren't in on your little script? What if they—oh, I don't know—*just kill you*? Then it's no Helena, no Helena's body, *and* no Antigone. Is that what you want? Because that's what it sounds like you're going to end up with. Just another corpse. Chalk another one up to your bull-headed stupidity."

"And what if I do die?" Antigone retorted. "Better for me that I should die in doing just that. That way, at least, I can be free of all this bullshit. The machinations of the astors, this insane exile from the only home I've known for these last seventy years. If they do kill me, at least it will all be over with. At least then I can rest. And when I do get to whatever hell is reserved for those of us who have sold our souls for this sad parody of life eternal, at least I will be able to face those I find there. I guess when it comes right down to it, I owe a greater allegiance to the dead than to the hollow rule of the living. In this world, I've overstayed my welcome, stretching out my tenure here for over a century. But in that world, I will live out the remainder of time. Better that I should be disloyal to the living than that I should dishonor our dead. But you, do what you will."

"I'm not 'dishonoring our dead,' Antigone. But to defy the Pyramid? After the events of these last weeks, I don't know that I've got the strength for such suicidal tasks anymore. I envy you your certainties, your conviction. But when you end up dead too, I'm not going back after your lifeless corpse either. I am not so eager to put your grand theories of the afterlife to the test. I will look to my own interests, here among the living."

"If that's your decision, fine. But I am glad that, of the two of us, it will be you who has to live with his choice. I am going to the chantry. Tonight."

"Don't tell me this," Johanus said in an exasperated tone.

"Why not? Will you feel obligated to turn me in? To call ahead to the chantry and tell them that I'm coming?"

"Of course not! I only meant that you have to be careful. Now more than ever. If you feel you have to do this—and I'd like to say, for the record, that this is probably the worst idea you've had to date. But if you have to do this, then at least have the good sense to keep quiet about it. If anybody should get wind of what you're going to do…"

"Shout it from the rooftops for all I care," she said, bitterly, "if you must hide here among the burned-out ruins of your ambitious plans. I, for one, never thought to see the night that your courage would not be equal to the task at hand. I would far rather you ran through the halls of the chantry proclaiming what I'm going to do. Your silence will only make me resent you more."

"Brave words," Johanus replied levelly. "But brave words do not make for brave deeds. Real bravery is the courage to take whatever misfortune heaps upon you, and to endure. To live on. You are rushing towards a coward's death, Antigone. If your intention is to kill yourself, better that you throw yourself into the flames here and now and have done."

"How is that going to help Helena?"

"You don't get it, do you? None of this is going to help Helena. This isn't even about Helena anymore. This is about the fact that you don't have what it takes to cope with being alone."

Antigone stood in silence for a time. Then she said, in a quiet voice, "I'm going now. Alone." She turned away from him and started back towards the basement stair.

"And what are you going to do, once you're inside, then?" he called after her. "Once you realize that you're in way over your head? There are some things, Antigone, that are just bigger and stronger than we are. The Pyramid is one of them."

She turned. "I've got to try, Johanus. Maybe you can't see that. And I guess I really can't be mad at you for it. And when my strength fails me, I'll know I did all I could. Helena believed in me. She trusted me. She gave me a chance. When she looked at me, she didn't see a failure, some vampiric misbirth, that even after half a century of struggle hadn't managed to master the bare rudiments of the blood arts. She made a place for me on her security team and pulled me out of a self-destructive spiral that I don't think I would ever have broken free of by myself. It was such a small gesture for her—as simple as giving me something productive that would occupy the sleepless hours. Something I was good at, damn it. Something to take my mind off the constant mockery of the other novices and the ritual of nightly self-condemnation. It was a tiny gesture for her, but one that made all the difference to me."

"Antigone..."

"I know I'm not likely to get beyond the front door, but I'm going to make the gesture. Do you understand?"

Johanus shook his head. "Is it so important that I understand?"

Her face fell. "No," she said quietly. "I don't suppose it is."

The silence hung heavy between them, broken only by the crackle of the fire. Johanus decided to make one more attempt.

"You don't have to do this, you know. It's a hopeless quest and no one—not even someone as judgmental as the dead—could hold you accountable if you just decided to just walk away."

Antigone's entire form seemed to stoop as if shrugging into a heavy pack. "Good bye, Johanus." Carefully she laid his keys on the desk and started up the stairs.

"Never could get anything through that head of yours," he muttered bitterly, more angry with his own failings than with hers. Then he called after her. "Look, Antigone, you know what I think of this idea, but for what it's worth..."

She turned, striking a pose just a bit belligerently.

"For what it's worth," he said, "the astors have changed all the security codes and protocols. You're never even going to get a chance to interface with the automated system, which I gather is what you did last time. That way's a death trap for you now."

Antigone frowned. Some of the hauteur went out of her stance. For just a moment, she was once again that gawky, uncertain novice coming to him for help. "What do you suggest?"

At the familiar note in her voice, he smiled, reminded of nights long ago. Of simpler, less dangerous times. For all of them.

"Direct approach," he said. "You walk right up to the main entrance and talk Talbott into opening the great portal for you. Talbott's a pussycat compared to what's waiting for you on the other side of those doors."

"Thanks," she said. Then, uncomfortably, "I'm sorry you're not coming with me. But I won't tell anyone that we've spoken."

"I'm sorry too, Antigone. And when this is all over—when the astors have gone again and the Chantry of Five Boroughs has a new regent and a clutch of new novices—I'll tell them all. About Sturbridge and Helena, about Anise and about you."

"Oh, Johanus," she said, and then fled back up the stairs.

Chapter Twenty-Seven
And Sings Itself to Sleep When All Is Done

The anteroom to the Chantry of Five Boroughs had something of the aspect of a luxurious private library about it. The floor-to-ceiling bookcases contained a multitude of scholarly texts rendered in the earthy tones of tooled leather, broken only by the sharp contrast of gilt edges.

The arrangement of books was precise if inutile. The volumes were grouped together by the simplest scheme that suggested itself—color. This approach encouraged a leisurely, disinterested browsing, and frustrated any attempts to discover any pertinent information. Frequent visitors to the chantry had grown bold enough to remark openly upon the curious and disproportionately heavy representation of the works of a Mr. Z. Grey among the shelves.

At the far end of the anteroom, beyond the ancient oak-paneled double doors—the two faithful and well-loved retainers leaned noticeably together upon sagging hinges—lay the grand foyer and chantry proper. The anteroom, however, was Talbott's private domain. He was the brother porter, the keeper of the gate, the guardian of the way. He had served the chantry faithfully for the better part of forty years.

During his tenure he had been witness to much of the mystery and majesty of the Tremere. Indeed, one could not spend so much time in the close proximity of the tumbledown great portal without seeing more than one's fair share of leaky incidental magics.

In all that time, however, of ushering supplicants, mystics, dignitaries and the occasional stray puppy across that formidable threshold, Talbott had never once passed through the great doors in their aspect of the portal of initiation. He had never once tasted of the forbidden fruit. "Never once been tempted," he could be overheard to boast contentedly to a dumbfounded guest. "No sir, never even been tempted."

But this was not the aspect of the room that Antigone loved best. She far preferred it on the nights when the trappings of the formal waiting room were shoved aside and relegated to the farthest corners. Once each month, Talbott, ever the incorrigible storyteller, held court over an enrapt group of novices, locals, old-timers, and a smattering of the more adventurous students from the college above.

A quiet footfall and a familiar voice broke in upon her fond recollections. "Well, you just lost me my stake," Talbott said, summoned from the stacks at the sound of the door opening and the inclement weather rushing in. "And that bottle of Powers would have been a welcome sight on a night such as this. But it's good to see you all the same. I thought for certain you were lost to us."

He came forward to take her by the arm and steer her down the three steps into the darkened interior of the hall. But Antigone hung back in the doorway.

"Estevez said to keep an eye out for you," Talbott continued. "Said that you'd be coming back this very night. Of course, I told him he hadn't half the sense the good Lord gave a goat. But here you are, our prodigal returned home to us. Well, there's nothing for it now but to come in out of the night, child. A night fit for neither man nor beast."

"Thank you, Talbott," Antigone said quietly. She glided down the steps, seeming to barely touch them. "I'm afraid that things inside promise to be even stormier. Has Estevez told you about…" the words caught in her throat, the lingering effect of the blood oaths she had sworn. "About why I've returned?"

"Not to me," Talbott grumped. "If he'd tipped his hand to me, I'd not be out that bottle. And I take it that I may have need of its comfort before the night's through."

She patted his arm. "You've always been kind to me," she began.

"Now, we'll have no talk of that kind. That's dead-man's talk. You've come to turn yourself back in, then? You'll forgive me saying so, but if you've come to throw yourself on the mercy of these *astors*," he spat the word like an invective, "it's going to take some doing to hit the mark. You'd have better luck throwing yourself off a building and hitting a thumbtack in the street below."

"Tried that," she replied. "Didn't work out. So here I am."

Talbott screwed up his brow and regarded her curiously. He knew she was pulling his leg, but her manner was deadpan and the circumstances of her return were something more serious. "If you want my advice—and I realize you're not asking it—I'd turn back around and get clean out of here before they realize you've even been. You've been away too long. You haven't seen the things that have been done here—and all in the name of the astors' *justice*. The words fail me; they turn to ashes and grave dirt in my mouth. When I think what they did to Anise and to Helena and to—"

"Take me to Helena."

Talbott regarded her levelly for a long while. He could see her resolve, that she would not be turned aside from this suicidal course. But he had to try. "Helena's beyond helping," he said. "You're not. Not yet, anyway. You walk through that door and you're lost. There's nothing for you in there but your own death, child. You listening to me? How's that going to help Helena, you dying?"

"Johanus said they've got her strung up. In the grand foyer. Like some kind of trophy." She was fighting a losing battle, struggling to simultaneously spit the words out while keeping her emotions in.

When Talbott finally met her eye, there was fire behind his gaze. Never before, during his entire tenure at the chantry, had Antigone seen the resentment and outrage burning openly there, boiling to the surface.

"Never again," he said flatly. "It ends here. Can't you see? Your going back in there only gives them another victim for their dark lusts—their hunger for blood, for terror, for suffering. Another lamb to the slaughter. You're only perpetuating the nightmare. Drawing it out, not only for yourself, but for everyone else in the chantry. Can't you just let them alone? Let them finish their casual brutalities so that they can leave? So that this nightmare will just be over?"

Antigone looked at him as if seeing him for the first time, with pity in her gaze.

She saw his face harden as her concern struck him like a physical blow. He drew himself up with pointed dignity, the rooster asserting his dominance at the door of the henhouse, feathers ruffling.

Antigone saw that she had hurt him, and hurt him casually. It was the last thing she wanted to do. To pick fights here, now. She looked upon him and saw only an old man, his hair gone thin and white from decades of guarding the threshold of the nightmare of the Tremere chantry. The door between the living and the dead. The mortal keeping watch over the gate of the undying.

He had done his job well, faithfully. But still, he was utterly beside the point. Powerless to stop the atrocities that he saw unfolding all around him. Powerless to voice an objection to them. Powerless even to flee the dark visions and run shrieking into the night.

Was that it? Antigone wondered. Was that the real heat behind Talbott's fiery resentment?

"Talbott, look, I'm sorry. Let's not argue. Not tonight of all nights. You may think that I can just turn around and walk out of here, but I can't. I'm as bound as you are. To this place, to the Pyramid. We've made our choices, sworn our oaths, offered up our sacrifices. We've got no choice—either of us—at this point, but to see this thing through. We're committed."

"We should be committed," he growled and then grew quiet. After a long while he spoke in a quiet voice, as if talking to himself. "I tried to leave. It was right after you had gone. Right after they... right after what they did to Anise." He fumbled over the words as if simply speaking them aloud would somehow make the atrocities come true again. Summon up something dark from the shadows that, for the moment at least, was satiated, at rest. Better left alone.

"I got as far as the freeway," he said. "Didn't have a penny to my name, of course, but that isn't what stopped me. I never had much use for spending money, really. Everything here has always been provided, just for the asking. I feasted like a king when the mood took me. I held court over a mile of books lined spine to spine. And at the clap of my hands, kegs of drink descended upon me for our little monthly gatherings. What did I want for money?

"I don't say these things to brag, but so you understand me when I say that I left this house with empty pockets and no more than the clothes on my back. Of course I was too proud to steal anything before I went. I left behind even those things that might well be considered as belonging to me, having been in my possession these forty years. Still, I had my wits and my tongue, and men have gone far in this world on far less.

"So this is what I did. I called up old Rafferty and asked him to come around. He's one of the locals, one who's wont to drop in from time to time. To share a pint and a tale, that kind of thing; a good sort, Rafferty. And I tell him I'm going up to Boston, on account of the fact that my sister has just passed, and could he see clear to giving me a lift up to the interstate so that I could start hitching a ride from there. On account of the fact that I didn't have a car of my own, you understand.

"Well, to his credit, he says he'll do me one better and drive me the whole way up and back. So I thank him kindly and tell him that I'm likely going to be staying a while with my sister's kids and that I can get a ride back with them in about week's time. He says that would be just fine and I figure I'm all set. Once I get to Boston, I'm sure that a crafty old Irishman can surely scrape by for a while, singing for his supper among the touristy spots."

Talbott paused, looking around ruefully for a mug ready to hand, but finding none.

"But you never made it to Boston." Antigone said.

"We got as far as the edge of the city. Rafferty's old LTD rattled fit to shake you loose of your bones. And the windows only rolled down about halfway. And the air conditioner didn't do much of anything except to puff the contents of the ashtray back up at you every time the car accelerated. But to me it was like standing at the bow of one of those grand old three-masted wooden sailing ships. Cleaving through the road ahead; throwing off a wake of pure possibility to either side.

"We stopped for gas at a BP station just north of the city proper. Because, Rafferty told me, the gas was eight cents cheaper there. I don't think he was fishing for gas money, but I didn't have any to offer him in any event, so I changed the topic. I told him I never remembered gas stations being so *bright* before. And it was, painfully bright. I squinted up trying to follow the series of arcane passes as Rafferty poked and prodded the pump to life. I watched the numbers on the pump writhe and change, almost too fast to follow. They settled on $17.25 and Rafferty said 'Come on,' and we went inside.

"Inside, if anything, was even brighter than outside. My head was already aching and I found myself looking forward to getting out on the interstate. The comforting vastness of the open road and the night sky.

"We grabbed some food and drinks for the trip. I let Rafferty sort through the bombardment of plastic and foil bags while I stuck to more familiar territory, the liquid refreshments. The guy behind the counter asked Rafferty for ID and I laughed out loud. 'Gotta ask,' the kid said defensively. 'It's the law.'

"The phone brayed at him as he was ringing up the sale. 'No. Nope. Nobody here named Talbott. Sorry.'

"My stomach dropped three inches. I looked out the plate-glass window and across the parking lot, and the big three-masted schooner was gone. In its place was only Rafferty's beat-up LTD, the muffler dragging on the pavement below it. You couldn't get anywhere in a car like that. Certainly not to Boston, much less all the way to a new start.

"Rafferty had his arm out for the phone, explaining things to the clerk. I imagine he was trying to help. He had to shout to make himself clear before the kid hung up the phone. As he got through, his tone became more level, eventually dropping to a pointed whisper. I picked out the words, 'His sister has just passed.' And the kid said, 'Passed what?' I reached for the phone.

"I put the receiver to my ear as if it were a gun. I heard the words coming over the line. I nodded in response, several times, not really caring that the person on the other end could not possibly see the gesture. My acquiescence was *understood*. Ahead of time.

"'I'm sorry,' I said to Rafferty. 'I've got to go back.' I don't even remember what I told him. Probably something about the arrangements being pushed back. Probably something about how one of my sister's kids would come down and pick me up this weekend. I don't know. Whatever the story was, he was polite enough on the way back not to press me on it. He dropped me off and told me if there was anything he could do to let him know.

"In the end I had to promise to at least get him the name of the funeral parlor. He actually sent flowers."

Talbott fell silent and sank into a nearby chair, all the resistance seeming to go out of his limbs. Antigone went over to him and laid a hand on his shoulder.

"I'm sorry," she said. "You deserve better."

"Better?" He gave a broken laugh. "I have it better here than I would trying to eke out a living hustling tourists in Boston. Far better. I have whatever I wish for, don't I? Three wishes for the storyteller. Jeweled rings, silken finery and ermine-trimmed robes—trappings fit for an emperor? Done. A river of ever-flowering ale? Nothing simpler. A magical harp that charms the birds from the sky, the maidens from their devotions, and sings itself to sleep when all is done? Done, done, and again done. There is no want here, Antigone. But I am no longer at all certain that freedom from want is something at all desirable. I find that without some level of want, there is no hope anymore. No aspiration towards the better. And that is the doorway of despair."

Antigone was silent a long while. "You and I," she said at last, "are dwellers upon the threshold. Gatekeepers, newlyweds, trolls beneath the bridge. Let us imagine that there is some doorway—a physical doorway—between hope and despair. Between living and dying. It is a doorway of volition. You may choose to act, to pass through the doorway, in either direction. You can walk through the chantry door for Boston, towards a new life. Or you can return to the familiar arms of the chantry, with all its gifts and faults, its bounty and its casual atrocities.

"For me the image is not so much that of a doorway, but of a precipice. You can walk out over the edge of the abyss, abandoning yourself to the inevitable, the bone-grinding drag of the world. Or you can soar out into nothingness in a blind leap of faith. It's not the direction of the passage that's important, but the intent. The act of volition. Is it a leap of hope or despair? Of anticipation or anxiety? I suspect your doorway may be much the same. You reentered the chantry in despair, having been called back, your wings clipped. I enter it in defiance, a rushing towards. The liberating difference is in the intent."

Talbott nodded. "Lecturing your elders is an unattractive habit in a young lady," he said, a slight smile spreading across his face. "You'll end up a spinster for certain."

"I, for one, would be delighted to end up an old anything," Antigone said. "I'm going in now. I hope you understand. Goodbye, Talbott."

Talbott pushed himself up laboriously from the chair. "Perhaps it's time I stretched my legs a bit as well," he said. "I've tried the outer door, didn't care for it much. Maybe I'll just see where that other door takes me."

Chapter Twenty-Eight
Pendulum Between Two Worlds

Talbott held the door wide for Antigone and stared after her retreating figure as she glided away from him across the grand foyer, knowing he would not see her again in this life.

Still he hung back, hovered at the very threshold of the Chantry of Five Boroughs. Before him, a mere footlength ahead, lay the grand foyer. But he could not bring himself to let that foot fall. On one side of the doorway were the comforts of his familiar domain. His books, his beer, his bed. On the other side, however, lay the chantry proper. Talbott was no stranger to the inside of the chantry house, but the presence of the astors had changed everything, casting an unsettling pall over the familiar surroundings.

Talbott knew that few outsiders had ever been granted the double-edged honor of setting foot within this particular domain of the warlocks. And fewer still could be persuaded to recount the tale of what they had found lying in wait for them there.

He also knew very well that a Tremere chantry was a place where all the terrors of what he called "the vampiric condition"—night and hunger, mystery and manipulation—were distilled down to their purest, most alluring and most lethal forms. The prospect of being invited to partake of this potent liqueur tantalized him at some primal level. It was a temptation that neatly evaded the defenses of judgment and intellect and went directly to work upon gullet, gut and groin.

Or perhaps the allure was something even more primeval. Yes, there was a hierarchy of desire at work here. That was certainly the message implicit in the Tremere's siren song—the never-ending chant of the chantry.

Between the desire and the spasm falls the shadow.

Talbott knew that there was some seat of desire that was deeper than the intellectual longing—the cravings to know, to understand, to master, to order, to arrange, to compose. Deeper even than the buried layer of the physical desires—the cravings for food, drink, warmth, sex. There was, beyond all these, a preeminent desire, an impulse of raw spirit. The reality of this desire broke upon him like a wave. It retreated a brief moment, only to crash over him again with redoubled force.

What a strange gift to place before strangers, here at the threshold.

As many times as Talbott had ushered guests through the grand foyer, the room had never seen fit to work its peculiar spell upon him, to present to him, in turn, its layered veils of desire and secrets. Something fundamental had changed. Something in his relationship to this house.

He saw his own desire laid bare before him. It was an aching to be whole once more. An undeniable urge to return home. An instinctive plunge towards unity, a longing towards belonging. Talbott was overwhelmed by the rough seduction of the threshold. Not the expected call to power, but a summons to oneness, an abandonment of self, a simultaneous annihilation and fulfillment.

Before him, the entry hall soared to dizzying heights. Its spires, galleries and sweeping stairways seemed to be rendered entirely in moonlight through stained glass. The delicate construct seemed wholly ephemeral. Talbott had the distinct and irrational conviction that if he were to blink the entire scene would dissolve and vanish from view.

The paths of the moonbeams streaming in through the colored glass seemed to have more substance than the walls and balustraded galleries of the grand foyer itself. Talbott could picture himself ascending the sharply sloping paths of light, climbing the treacherous slope to the very pinnacle of desire.

But some distant part of his mind held him back from abandoning himself to this alien communion of power and desire. There was a sinister edge to that promise. And a sense that, once he crossed this threshold, he might not be able to cross back.

Talbott glanced behind him, checking the way back. A wave of vertigo swept over and staggered him. For a moment, he had the distinct impression that the grand foyer lay not before him, but behind. He wheeled suddenly back towards his only avenue of escape and found himself, once again, facing the vast, moonlit hall.

Talbott began to turn again and then thought better of it. He forced himself to remain calm, closing his eyes until little more than a faint impression of light and shadow reached him through the slit of his eyelids.

Cautiously, with tentative shuffling steps, he tested his new conviction. It was as he feared. Neither forward nor back; neither advance nor retreat was open to him. It was as if he were caught fast in the complex web of desires that the chantry wove about him.

Time stretched uncomfortably. Talbott expected at any moment that his resignation would give way to the cold rush of panic. He was puzzled that, instead, his utter powerlessness brought with it a rather cool clarity of thought.

It is most likely that I am about to die. That was his first thought. Talbott regarded the idea without fear, but with a certain curiosity, even anticipation. He rolled it around on his tongue, finding it cool, firm, sweet. Absently he wondered how, after forty years of service here, upon this very threshold, he thought he would ever be able to leave it.

Antigone wasn't sure why the grand foyer didn't react to her presence, throwing up its familiar barriers of temptations and condemnations. Perhaps it was because the things she feared and desired most were both already awaiting her, just inside.

She barely noticed the other figures in the room. She drifted through them like a ghost, not even touching them or ruffling their garments as she passed. Her attention was fixed on the *diagramma* at the center of the hall.

Helena hung, suspended and inverted, directly before the ancient fountain that was the focal point of the hall in all of its incarnations.

Antigone strode right up to the edge of the diagram that encircled the adept, her toes nearly brushing the chalk line, but she dared come no farther. Even from this proximity, she could not tell if Helena had survived the astors' ministrations. The adept's flesh was as pale and transparent as onion paper—as if she had been totally exsanguinated. Only once before had Antigone seen someone with so little blood in his body, and that novice had been whipped into a ravening frenzy by the hungers of the Beast.

Helena hung absolutely motionless. If she wasn't yet fully dead, the vital spark was now somewhere so far removed that not even the thrashings of the Beast could touch her anymore. She was either truly dead or deep into the bloodless slumber of torpor—deeper than Antigone had ever seen before.

The only assurance that the adept had not met her final death was that her body remained intact. Helena was older than Antigone. She had spent well over a century and a half flouting the powers of death and decay. If she had truly met her end, these powers would have savaged her remains—reducing her to a pile of decayed flesh and yellowed bones within a matter of minutes.

Then a darker thought occurred to her. Perhaps the purpose of the unfamiliar diagram that contained the adept was simply to preserve her remains, not the faint flicker of her half-life. That it was less medical than taxidermic.

Antigone studied the supporting glyphs that circumscribed the diagram, but they refused to surrender any of their secrets. As she leaned in closer, she was startled by a hissing noise, and jumped backwards. A faint pink mist drifted up from the diagram. It soon filled the circle, arcing to form a dome above the adept—its apex, the point where the chain binding her feet emerged from the ceiling.

There was no mistaking the sanguine nature of the mists. The heady aroma of vitae slapped Antigone across the face. For a moment, she had the unsettling impression that the dome of diffused blood formed a bell jar containing the curious specimen that had once been Helena.

A strangled animal sound escaped Antigone's throat, an inarticulate cry of horror, of outrage. To think that they could do such a thing! And to Helena, whose only crime had been a century of service to this very house.

"Steady," whispered a voice directly behind her. "Mustn't let them see it when they've hurt you."

Antigone wheeled, an angry retort on her lips, but it died when she found herself facing Estevez. His warning only threw her into further confusion. "But they… look what they've…"

Estevez did not outwardly acknowledge Antigone's outburst in any way. His voice was kept in tight check, pitched low so as not to be overheard. His eyes never left the dangling adept and even his lips barely moved. "It is a *defilement*," he hissed. "To keep her hanging here like this, swinging like a pendulum between the living and the dead…"

"Stop it!" Antigone shouted up into his face.

At her shout, heads turned towards them. A look of disappointment flickered across Estevez's face. Then he turned to her with a look of surprise, as if noticing her for the first time. When he spoke, his voice now carried clearly across the room. The earlier note of compassion was suddenly gone from it.

"Novitia! I am glad you have decided to keep our appointment. You have done the right thing, have no fear on that account. Turning yourself in is really the best thing you could have done in these circumstances."

"I didn't come here to turn myself in. I came here to—" She started to say something about the *certámen* challenge, but the words physically stuck in her throat. The damned blood oath again.

"Yes, of course," Estevez quickly interrupted. "To face your accusers, to clear your name. Well, it amounts to much the same thing, yes?"

His quip was met with amusement from around the room, which quickly dissolved into a scattered and self-conscious titter. Few present were anxious to be seen openly criticizing the astors' justice in even this slight way.

This wasn't right at all, Antigone thought angrily. Then, for the first time, she seemed to take in her surroundings more fully. Estevez had not prepared any of the trappings for the *certámen*. Where were the nested protective circles of the rite?

"What's going on here, Eugenio?" she demanded.

"I assure you, I am as surprised by this development as you are," he said. He spoke with exaggerated slowness, his eyes boring into hers as if he could drive understanding home to her simply by the force of his stare. "Still, I'm sure the astors had their reasons for making such a… startling example of the adept. Certainly, no one is questioning that there is a wrong here that must be addressed."

"I don't understand," she muttered. Was Estevez saying that Helena had done something deserving of such a fate? Or that the wrong that had been committed was that of the astors? It just didn't click together for her. "What could Helena have done to deserve this?!"

Estevez let the question hang. At last he said, "I made similar inquiries. I am told that she killed a novice, conspired to undermine the astor's judgments and betrayed her regent."

"That's a crock!" Antigone said. "Helena would never do any of that stuff."

The hall had grown silent.

"Under normal circumstance," Estevez said cautiously, "I would be inclined to agree. Apparently, these are not normal circumstances."

"I don't believe this. This isn't right! Helena didn't do any of those things and if she did, she still didn't deserve anything like this! I'm getting her down from there, right now." She started back towards the diagram.

"That would not be wise," Estevez put in hastily. "Perhaps you are unfamiliar with that particular *diagramma hermetica*. There is a death trapped within it. A death that has been stolen from the adept. It would be very foolish indeed to cross that line."

Antigone stopped, just short of the chalk circle. Without turning back to him she asked, "Are you saying that it would kill Helena?"

"I am saying that if you were to release it, it might not be very particular about who it struck down. It has been frustrated and kept at bay overlong. And you would be placing yourself directly in its path."

Antigone scowled down at the sigils that ringed the diagram, trying to puzzle out their meaning. She could not tell how far Estevez could be trusted, even in this. For some reason, he too seemed upset about finding Helena like this. But he certainly had a funny way of showing it. A more circumspect way. And she was tiring of his insinuations and veiled manipulations.

"Look, you know why I came here tonight. Now are we going to have this out or—"

"Easy, novitia. Yes, I know why you have come here." He placed a hand upon her shoulder and she shuddered at his touch. "You wish to offer me formal challenge, here in front of the entire chantry. Is that not so?"

A muted commotion ran through the room. Antigone, in response, nodded. She did not trust her voice to obey her. Estevez took hold of her other shoulder and held her there, so that she could not turn away from Helena. "I just wanted to make sure," he said, "that you fully understood what is at stake here tonight."

In a harsh whisper, inaudible to the rest of the onlookers, he said, "You are going to die here tonight, Antigone. But you are going to die so that nothing like this," he gripped her shoulders more painfully, almost shoving her in the direction of Helena, "ever happens here again."

"I don't see how my death is going to…"

"Your death," Estevez said in her ear, "or rather, the fact that you are still among the living, is all that's keeping these bastards here. It's all they've been doing these past two weeks — trying to track you down. Now, I don't know where you've been, although I've got some suspicions. And I don't really care. All that matters now is that these bastards can't go back to the Fatherhouse and report that they've left a renegade dark thaumaturge at large. Sturbridge's report on that little incident between you and Stephens soured the whole deal for everybody. They can't ignore it, they can't pretend it didn't happen, they can't leave. You understand?"

"I get it," she said, shrugging free of him. "I've got to die and I've got to die here, in front of witnesses."

"There really isn't any other way."

"And what do you get out of all of this? A medal? You've got to get some credit for bringing me in, I guess. And it's a snub in the face of the astors if they've been trying as desperately to find me as you make out. And I guess killing me in some flashy magical duel is worth something. It will leave a memorable impression at least...."

"That part was your idea, not mine."

"All right then, let's just do this thing."

Estevez nodded and turned to speak with a novice who was standing nearby. He was only gone for a few minutes, but to Antigone, the time stretched agonizingly. She tried to arrange her thoughts, to summon up the necessary resolve to do what she must. If they wanted a death from her, she would give them a death.

Antigone was no stranger to the theatric nature of death. In a way, she had been preparing for this all her nights. The final dramatic exeunt. Six times she had staged her daring raids into the realm of the dead, and six times she had danced away again unscathed with a flourish and a bow. The sharp snap of the matador's cape, the roar of the crowd.

She was born to play this part and she would give them all their money's worth.

The novice returned with the necessary trappings, bent under the weight of the bundle. He settled his burden to the floor with a thump and Estevez, a master showman in his own right, set to unpacking the big top.

Chapter Twenty-Nine
Certámen

E stevez extracted a black drawstring pouch and, loosening the cord at its neck, shook out some of the contents into the palm of his hand. Antigone could see the gritty substance consisted of a hasty admixture of ash and old bone with chunks of some more pungent material thrown in. Estevez rolled the mixture around in his hand, testing its texture. Satisfied, he grunted and upended the entire sack over a beaten copper basin that the novice—Antigone thought his name was Jason, but she could not remember—held at arm's length.

As Estevez turned away, the novice gritted his teeth and opened a wide cut in his forearm, letting his blood slide down the rough side of the basin to mingle with the grisly mixture. He then worked it with his bleeding hand, like a baker kneading dough.

While the novice worked, Estevez busied himself with pacing off a cleared area ten paces in diameter and shooing back the curious spectators that crept within this domain for a closer look. He accepted the copper basin in solemnity and silence, tipping down its lip ever so slightly. A trickle of thick gloppy liquid spilled over the brink and splashed to the floor.

Estevez worked quickly, walking in a brisk circuit around the cleared area, trailing the noxious mixture behind him as he went. Only when he had completed the full circuit did he look up to survey his handiwork. He smiled.

It was, as best as Antigone could determine, a perfect circle, painted in soot and ash and fallen lifeblood. She doubted that she could have done half so well, even if the outline had been measured out beforehand and marked on the floor in chalk.

Antigone found herself put in mind of a story about the Renaissance artist, Raphael, being summoned to his first audience with the pope. When Raphael was introduced, he launched immediately into such a spiel of braggadocio that the pope was moved to put him to the test at once. Accordingly he called for a brush and a small pot of purple paint, which he presented to the self-proclaimed maestro, that he might show them a masterpiece. Raphael did not hesitate, but immediately rendered a perfect circle on the floor at the foot of the papal throne. Raphael so impressed the pontiff that he secured his future livelihood.

To top his own feat, Estevez poured out two more circles within the first, each two paces across. These would be the positions from which the combatants faced off.

"If you are ready," he said, gesturing to the empty ring nearest her, "you may begin your preparations."

Estevez took up his own position and bent down to scratch some arcane symbols around the perimeter in chalk.

Hesitantly, Antigone stepped over the line and into her own circle. She watched Estevez for some moments before she realized that the novice—Jason?—was standing beside her, holding out a small cushion on which rested chalk, candles and a stiletto. She accepted these and thanked him, but he was impassive. Perhaps she had called him by the wrong name after all.

Estevez was just completing his own diagram when Antigone knelt to sketch the first shaky supporting glyphs of her own. She was clearly out of her league here. She racked her brain to remember some of the protective diagrams she had seen in the pages of the *Spiritus Mundi* or *Pythoras Trismagerus*, but she couldn't seem to remember any of the wardings in their entirety. And a partial—or worse, incorrectly rendered—diagram was not only useless, it was often dangerous as well.

She felt Estevez's eyes on her and she became more flustered than ever, imagining his smug grin, the exaggerated tapping of one foot. She stooped and started scratching around the circle, rendering whatever glyphs she could call to mind.

She was a quarter turn around the circle before she realized the pattern she was recreating. The only diagram she had ever successfully invoked—the protective circle inverted. The diagram that she had glimpsed only briefly in the crypts beneath the chantry. The one she had unwisely used in her attempt to slow down the pursuing astor atop the widow's walk. The pattern that Sturbridge had identified as a forbidden dark thaumaturgic rite.

There was a muttering from the gathered onlookers as questions and conjectures were passed from ear to ear through the crowd. She doubted whether any of the novices present could have guessed the true intent of this unorthodox configuration of symbols. She wasn't entirely certain of its purpose herself.

She knew that the other time she had used this containment diagram, it had effectively imprisoned Stephens, cutting him off in the middle of an attempted apportation. Neither Stephens nor Antigone had been physically able to pass the barrier and even sound could not permeate it. Although Antigone was not entirely certain that she liked the thought of voluntarily locking herself within such a diagram, she hoped that the barrier might repulse some of Estevez's mystic assaults. And, to tell the truth, she was already too far committed at this point to try to turn back now and start a new diagram—even if she could remember one.

Hoping for the best, Antigone arranged the last supporting glyph, and the circle was complete. Only then did she look up to face Estevez and see the look of perplexity—and was it perhaps a hint of amusement?—on his face.

His own preparations were long since completed. Antigone glanced down at them somewhat self-consciously. She did not like the look of some of those sigils he had marshaled to his defense. She was fairly certain that the foremost squiggle, which seemed to writhe on its own in the dim light, was some obscure conjugation of the elemental rune of fire. That was very bad news. Even the most basic pyromantic defenses had eluded Antigone throughout her studies. If Estevez could drive the conflict into that arena, it would be over very quickly.

Some of the other glyphs seemed familiar. She could pick out the runes for the major blood manipulations—healing, stamina, symbiotic transfer, empathetic bleeding—there were many others, and even the ones she felt comfortable with boasted unsettling serifs and embellishments which left her guessing after the true nature of their obviously sinister intent.

It was then that Antigone had one of those rare intuitive flashes that are summoned up only in times of direst life-threatening crisis. She had been puzzling over the individual glyphs in Estevez's diagram for some time; then, in a searing flash, she understood the meaning behind, not the individual components, but the entire diagram. It broke upon her with a cool certainty, and there was no doubting its message or avoiding its consequences. The diagram could not have been clearer or more eloquent if it had spoken to her aloud. It said, "You are going to die."

Now, Antigone was not afraid of death. She had foolishly gone rushing towards it as many times as she had run away from it. But there was something different this time. The certainty of it. The inevitability.

She had spent her existence flirting with many little deaths. With ledges, pills, and gas ovens. Now, for the first time, she found herself facing the reality of the totality of her death, the concept of her non-existence. It rattled her and she found herself afraid, perspiring a dainty sheen of red-tinged droplets.

Estevez saw the change come over her. Saw her growing realization, smelled her sickly sweet fear. "Shall we begin?"

Suddenly Antigone wanted to do anything but begin. She wanted to fidget with her protective circle, she wanted to bolt from the nested circles.

"Ah, I almost forgot," he said. Antigone latched onto the sound of his voice as if it were a life preserver. "I promised you a third condition for our contest. Do you remember? Good. The final condition is this: no manmade objects—no artifacts, foci. Nothing but the dark majesty of the blood."

He handed the chalk to the novice who attended upon him, just outside the circles. Then he removed his wristwatch and handed that over as well.

Antigone stared at him blankly for a moment before she seemed to realize what was expected of her. She patted absently at her pockets. Then, unslinging her bag from her shoulder, she began dropping objects into it. Before long, she had chalk, candles, an oversized straight razor. And Felton's .45 caliber army-issue pistol.

Reluctantly, she handed the entire lot over to Jason when he crossed to her side of the circle. Jason whistled low at the impressive array of firepower and cold steel. She cursed silently, realizing that any of these things might have proved of some advantage in a contest in which she was likely to have few if any points in her favor.

"If you are ready, novitia?"

Antigone nodded, and immediately Estevez's hands came up in invocation. They paused only a fraction of a second at the crux of their arc before flashing down again. The glyph of fire surged in response. Two great gouts of flame shot out, one from his right side, one from his left. Where the roaring flames contacted the outer circle there was a metallic screeching and the fire reared and turned, following the circle's arc.

Two waves of fire, each the mirror image of the other, curled and broke over Antigone. She felt the weight of them crash down upon her. The force of the air pushed before them drove her to one knee. She awaited the hot rush of pain, the smell of searing flesh, the laughing cackle of flames dancing along skin. But the blow did not fall.

Glancing up, Antigone saw herself encapsulated in a dome of fire. The flames strove against the protection of her inverted circle, but could not prevail against it. For the moment, at least. Still, the heat inside her cocoon was growing unbearable in itself.

Antigone wasn't sure quite what to do next. Her plan hadn't extended any further than following Estevez's example in throwing up a protective circle and hoping for the best. She did not have any idea how to shoot bolts of fire or lightning or anything like that. She had no means of seizing the offensive, of striking back.

In desperation, she tried to will the flames to turn back towards Estevez. She threw up her arms dramatically and uttered an invocation in Latin, concentrating as hard as she could on turning aside the deadly canopy of fire.

Nothing happened.

Antigone was suddenly thankful for the engulfing roar of flames. She could picture the other novices looking on, laughing at her silly and pitiful attempts. The indignity of it stung and she wanted to sink from sight. To let the wall of flames crash down upon her, burying her from sight. Snuffing out the small, fragile spark of her existence by the overwhelming bulk of its own fire. To lose herself, to abandon all thought of self within the vast sea of flame, just as she had once eclipsed herself within the horizon-encompassing arms of the ocean. To go down. To drown. To be still.

Antigone found herself thrashing about, almost against her will, struggling for the surface, kicking out desperately. Somewhere above her, there was air, there was breath, there was life. But she had been so long beneath the dark waters now that she no longer knew which way was up. Or even why such things as breath and life, so long left behind her, were even important anymore.

She felt herself curling inward upon herself like the corner of a manuscript page held to a candle flame. Elbows upon knees, face upon hands, curling. Inward. She found herself tumbling through dark turgid waters.

Antigone found herself at the brink of a silent well, staring down into the dark waters. She knew this place. She had seen it a hundred times before in a hundred different nightmares. Against her will, she found herself drawn closer. She closed her eyes and reached out a hand to touch the surface of the water, knowing what was sure to follow. The sudden disturbance of the placid surface. The clammy blue hand of the drowned child reaching up to grab her wrist. To pull her down.

She screamed and broke from the troubling inner visions, kicked away from the old nightmare. *Not here!* she thought. *Not now.* But the chill of those subterranean waters still clung to her. Even as Antigone opened her eyes upon the nightmare of flames, she found herself shivering with the cold and damp.

And as Antigone rose back to the surface of consciousness, something of that benighted tarn rose with her. The flames shrank back before it, reluctant to touch it and be quenched in its icy depths. Antigone thought she knew exactly how they felt.

184 / Eric Griffin

There was a time, long ago, when that well had meant something very different to her. It was her silent place, her still point. When she was a young woman, it was the place where she gathered her most prized treasures. Alone, in the isolation of her room in Scoville, Antigone would turn out all of the lights, pull down the shades, and stuff a blanket under the door. Then, when the outer dark was absolute, indistinguishable from the inner blackness, she would dive into those inky depths of her own consciousness.

She could remember how it felt cutting through the icy waters, holding her breath and fighting for the bottom of the well. In those depths, everything extraneous fell away—stray thoughts, nagging perceptions, even awareness of self. The trick was to reach the bottom before she blacked out. To grab for the images and insights scattered there, at her very core, beneath thought, beneath knowing.

When she succeeded, she would kick out for the surface with her hard-won jewel and frantically scribble it down into her book of poems before it could wriggle free from her grip. Groping for her fountain pen in the dark, feeling the words take shape, as if they were written in braille. All the while buoyant with her find, exuberant and treading water.

But all that had changed long before she was ushered over the threshold of the undying. Her poetry notebooks were probably still there, at the bottom of a trunk in the corner of a basement in Scoville. Treasures resting forgotten at the bottom of some damp, stone-walled well.

But by the time she had grown to a woman, she had put such childish things behind her. And then came the War, and the Army Signal Corps and Paris! And then after the War, there was the job on the telephone switchboard, and then David and then marriage. And with one thing and another she forgot all about the well, and its dark majesty and the brilliant treasures that lurked on its gravelly bottom.

It was the first week after her Embrace into this nocturnal existence that the nightmares had started. She remembered coming in slumber, as if by chance, upon the brink of the familiar well. It was like meeting an old friend from childhood. She found herself wandering through her old room, just touching all her old things. They all seemed so tiny to her now, so delicate. The silver hairbrush, the glass-and-gold inkwell from the Orient, the fountain pen. All seemed like furnishing from a dollhouse. She was half afraid that the things would snap in two in her hands, or tumble from the desk and shatter at her tread.

She soon found herself going through the steps of her old ritual (lights off, shades down, blanket under door) and plunging down into primal inner darkness. The shock of the icy water seemed a slap across the face, a denial. The waters themselves tried to outmaneuver her, to block her path to the icy depths.

She struck out, kicked off for the bottom, but immediately bumped *into* something. She groped blindly in front of her and felt the unmistakable outline of cold, pudgy fingers.

Antigone screamed, swallowing lungfuls of the turgid black waters and awoke in her bed in the novice *domicilium*, gasping desperately for air she no longer technically needed.

That was her first encounter with the Children Down the Well. In the weeks and years to come, she would return to the sight of that first encounter time and time again. Each time, she found the bloated blue-skinned bodies had pressed closer to the surface, clamoring ever upward upon each other's shoulders, borne surfaceward by the sheer mass of victims beneath them.

It soon came to be a place Antigone instinctively shied away from. Soon the faces of the drowned started to take on familiar aspects. Antigone could pick out the features of each and every victim she had fed from over the decades. And there were still so many others, countless others, clamoring for attention. She had come to dread their nocturnal visits, even as she came to know the confined space of their slumbering world as well as the confinement of her waking one, within the walls of the Chantry of Five Boroughs.

And so it was that Antigone immediately knew that something was different this time. Something was amiss. Under the relentless pressure of Estevez's assault, Antigone found herself forced to retreat, driven back to that last inner shore. But something there was missing. Immediately she knew what it was. The Children—they were gone.

She realized intellectually of course that they had been missing for weeks now, ever since the night Sturbridge had been found in the crypts. But the implications of that fact had not sunk in until now. If the Children were gone, the well was hers again—its welcome oblivion, its sunken wonders.

Even as Estevez's fiery attack peeled away before the touch of the chill waters, Antigone was diving again. Kicking down into the depth. Groping in the darkness. There.

What was so startling to her was that she had tested the waters and, for the first time since she had entered this benighted existence, there was no fear there. No reproach.

That was Sturbridge's doing, Antigone thought. She had taken the Children away, swallowed them. Sturbridge was their scapegoat, Antigone realized with sudden clarity. The one who had taken all the sins of their people upon her back, like bundles of sticks. The regent had bent beneath the weight and broken. But who would not have? Who could hope to shoulder all the recriminations, to face all their collective accusers, all their victims?

The Children were the dark obverse of the terrifying power inherent in the Tremere blood. They were its safeguard, its conscience. And Sturbridge had taken all that away.

Cautiously, Antigone tested the waters once more. She still half expected to see the serene faces bobbing there, their hair spread out across the surface of the waters like fishing nets, their eyes—round and bright as moons—staring up at her. Imploring. But no ripple disturbed the dark waters.

Some distant part of her mind was still aware of what was going on outside, far removed from her inner sanctum. Estevez, frustrated that his attack had broken against the clumsy defenses of a mere novice, was mustering his forces for something truly horrendous. She saw him tap into the elemental rune of fire once more, but this time it was a mere accent color as he dipped time and again into several of the glyphs of the primal blood magics. The air before him seethed and crackled. With a shout, Estevez jabbed the nascent energies down into an unfamiliar glyph that resembled nothing more than a serpent swallowing its own tail, forming a complete protective circle in miniature. Antigone did not have much time to puzzle over the meaning of the obscure symbol. The force of the roiling energies that Estevez brought crashing down upon the sigil ruptured it. It uncoiled with a crack of mystic energy that sent a ripple through the marble floor directly towards Antigone.

The novice had no time to react, to try to summon up her defenses. Without thinking, she took the only option open to her—escape. Drawing a deep breath, a vestigial habit from a lifetime ago, she dove into the well.

The pulsing wave of marble crashed into the edge of Antigone's inverted circle and erupted.

The supporting glyphs shattered with the sound of breaking glass. One end of her protective circle burst loose and sprang up off the floor like a high-tension cable suddenly severed. The opposite end whipped around with enough force to slice anyone who had been standing within arm's reach in two.

The loose ends writhed and snaked upwards, turning upon Antigone. They coiled around her again and again, entwining themselves around and between her limbs. They attacked with the speed and ferocity of twin serpents, flaring up and weaving a deadly helix of blood and fire around her. Antigone screamed, feeling flesh sear and bones break beneath the ever-tightening grip of her own *diagramma* turned against her.

She thought that she must appear like some twisted mockery of the caduceus, the twin serpents wrapped around a staff. A sign of healing and solace. The caduceus was the scepter of the Roman god Mercury, she thought absently, the messenger god. The spokesman for Hades and the go-between between the living and the dead.

But at the same time that she was aware of her body being savaged by the twin serpents of blood and fire, another part of Antigone, a younger, more fragile part, was kicking frantically for the safety and oblivion of the watery depths. Somewhere just ahead there was the cool silence of the still-point. A place free from the pain, the humiliation, the failure of the outer world. A place free from senses, free from thought.

She remembered the way as clearly as if it had been the space of a mere day separating her forays into this dark inner realm, instead of a span of decades. Far above, her body writhed in searing pain and would have crumpled to the floor had it not been for the vice-like grip of the attack holding her upright. Then her powerful strokes brought her to a place where she lost all awareness of the agony, all sensation from the outer world. Her last impression was of the expression on Estevez's face as he saw the spark of resistance go out of her. Not a look of exultation, but rather one of resignation and perhaps even regret. Then all was darkness.

It was some time later—whether a minute, an hour, a year, it was impossible to measure—that Antigone gradually became aware of the sensation of something sharp cutting into her cheek. She tried to brush it away but her hands only buried themselves to the knuckles in slime-thick gravel. With the sluggishness and reluctance of someone emerging from deep sleep, Antigone realized that she was lying at the bottom of the well. Her groping hands probed through the shifting stones until they found solid purchase, and then she pushed herself up onto her elbows. The jagged stone that had been cutting into her face must have fallen away, although she could see nothing in the complete darkness.

As she levered herself back up to a sitting position, she was startled when her groping hand brushed against something smooth and—most disturbingly—warm among the tangle of slime and sharp edges that composed the well's bottom.

She grabbed for it and it slipped her grasp twice before her fingers closed around it. It was no larger than the palm of her hand, flat and smooth like a skipping stone. She couldn't pick out any other details here in the darkness, so she kicked off the bottom and surged upwards towards the surface.

Antigone erupted from the well, her upraised fist blazing like a sun but emitting an ebon light that burned with chill instead of heat. The twin serpents reared back, hissing and sputtering. Antigone screamed and doubled over convulsively as the awareness of pain came flooding back to her. There was the fire in her chest of broken ribs, and a hollow whistling in the rasping scream that spoke of a punctured lung. Desperately, she willed blood to the broken and battered parts of her body. But her injuries were extreme, perhaps mortal. Certainly far more extensive than her reserve of life-giving vitae.

The dark fire clenched in her fist flared, and the twin serpents flinched away from it, their scales grating over each other with a metallic sound in their haste to disentangle themselves.

They were not fast enough. The arcane energies that held them together frayed and split. They collapsed to the floor in a puddle of gore and spent ashes.

Estevez gaped. He had thought the novice dead already. He did not know how she had survived this onslaught. Up until that moment, he had not known it was even possible to survive it. He could not imagine what was keeping her on her feet. And he did not like the look of the dark energy she had summoned up.

He let the attack dissolve back into its primal energies and hastily nudged his defenses to life. A glyph flared a warding against diabolic interventions.

He needn't have bothered. The expected counter-attack never materialized. Instead, the dark power surged once more, and Antigone collapsed to the floor.

Chapter Thirty
Exeunt

From some inner wellspring, Antigone eventually found the strength to rise again. She rolled to one side and pushed herself up onto elbows and knees.

Estevez gaped at her. He raised his arms for one final fiery invocation, but there was no answering flare from the elemental glyphs arrayed around him. Antigone had broken the circle, fallen across the boundary. The contest was over. The invested magics had drained from the *diagramma*.

For a moment, he almost lashed out at her from sheer frustration. Even without the ·*certámen* circles to magnify his powers, Estevez still could have opened a vein, drawn directly on the power inherent in his Tremere blood to bring down a fiery coup de grâce.

It was only with great effort that he reigned in the hungering Beast within. The monstrous cobra flared its hood and reared higher than a man. Estevez felt the trill of its tongue testing the air, finding the soft spot just beneath the line of his jaw. He felt, rather than heard, the snap as the serpent's jaw unhinged, its maw gaping to monstrous proportions—wide enough to take Estevez's entire head in its jaws.

Very slowly, Estevez lowered his arms. He knew that between the two foes—the fallen novice and the incarnation of his own deadly hungers—he now faced the more dangerous adversary. He was not so foolish as to try to tackle the monstrous viper head-on. A serpent had to be coaxed, courted, mesmerized.

Without breathing or moving a muscle, using no more than his gaze and the trained will behind it, Estevez began the seduction—soothing the aroused viper, easing it back into the roiling snake pit from which it had emerged.

Antigone tried to rise to her feet and failed miserably, slumping to the floor again in a heap. She rolled to her right and saw that she now lay directly between the two *diagramma*—the *certámen* circles and the bell-jar warding which contained the gently swinging adept.

Then there was a gap in her perceptions; she might have blacked out for a moment. She blinked trying to focus on Helena's features, the adept's head stared down at her unseeing. Dangling only a few handbreadths away. She imagined she could almost reach up and...

There was a hand on her elbow. An unfamiliar voice was muttering in hushed tones, "I said, can you stand? Are you all right?" She tried to turn towards the sound but instantly regretted it. In the moment before the pain took her, she saw that it was the novice. Jason? He was trying to help her sit up, holding something in his other hand, shielding it with his body from the sight of the other spectators. Something that gleamed blue black in the uncertain light. Like gunmetal.

She tried to focus on the gun, the primary threat. But she kept stumbling over all the secondary ones—the broken ribs, the punctured lung, the loss of blood. The awareness of Estevez, hovering somewhere nearby. The avaricious press of the spectators, their own hungers all too plain on their faces, clamoring for the mercy stroke.

She squinted, trying to keep the barrel of the gun in focus, but failing. She closed one eye and then the other, but no matter how she stared, she still wasn't facing down the business end of the barrel. The gun seemed to be tucked in close to his own chest, lying flat against his robes.

Jason prodded her in the ribs with the weapon and she doubled over anew, certain she had been shot save for lack of the retort of the pistol. Perhaps she had gone deaf as well, reopened her punctured eardrum in the clash of arcane energies.

"Take it, idiot!" he hissed, pressing the gun directly into her hand this time.

"I don't... I don't understand," she muttered. She felt the cool metal against her badly burned skin, but her fingers refused to close around the stock.

"I'm offering you a way out. Take it. Quickly!"

Her index finger curled around the trigger guard; she fumbled for the safety.

Suddenly a cry went up from the nearest spectator. "Gun! Stop her!" He started to surge forward and then, seeing that others around him did not share his idea, he faltered. The novice at his side gave him a condescending look and pointedly stepped back out of the firing line.

Jason pretended to wrestle with her for the gun. Antigone doubted his efforts were convincing. She hadn't the strength to resist him. Where he tugged the gun went; where he pushed it followed.

"Damn Estevez! He should have killed you. He knew what the astors would do to you if you survived the *certámen!*"

Suddenly Antigone realized the true extent of her predicament. She had narrowly escaped a fiery death in the arcane duel, only to face an even more unpleasant one at the hands of the astors. *The judgment of my peers,* Antigone thought. She was overcome, not by fear, but by an overwhelming feeling of failure. This was the judgment she had asked for. That she had *demanded* of the jackal god. Out of the corner of her eye, Antigone caught sight of Helena's cold and bloodless body

194 / Eric Griffin

gently penduluming through the air. For a moment, she thought she could detect in the adept's face, in the translucent skin drawn parchment thin over a leering skull, a trace of the Cheshire-cat smile of the laughing guardian of the dead.

The gun loomed into view, pressed for a moment against the flesh of her forehead and Jason's earnest whisper. "Now! For Christ's sake, do it now!"

Antigone closed her eyes and sank to her knees. She felt the trickle, wet with blood sweat. "I'm sorry," she said and squeezed. The report echoed through the high hall, bringing with it the smell of spent power and newly spilled blood. No one moved.

Jason slumped to the floor. A ragged hole torn through the front of his raven-black novice robes was quickly tinting them with dark red.

Several other novices began easing away from her. She waved the gun menacingly at one who edged just a bit to close to her in his effort to get away. Caught in this compromising position, he drew himself up, striking a pose in a display of eleventh-hour bravado. The shot caught him square on, picking him clean up off the floor and sending him tumbling over backward into the fountain, where he lay still.

Some of the novices were calling for a security team, but either the comm port had been locked down or the security daemon was off-line again. Antigone found herself wondering who, if anyone, on the security crew was left to answer that call, even if it did go out. *Probably just the astors,* she thought. This realization brought her back to the immediacy of her surroundings. She couldn't be caught here. Not like this. Not before she had done what she had come here to do.

Calming herself and forcing down dueling pains in her chest that clamored for her attention, Antigone reached down to touch that dark silent pool within her. The wellspring of the power of the Tremere blood. Gone now was the fear represented by the Children, the check on her summoning up the blood magics.

Working quickly and intuitively, she bent to the supporting glyphs around the circle that surrounded Helena, that kept her chained between life and death. She subtly altered a supporting glyph here, struck out a binding there, and then paused over the primal rune, the one that was the focus of the *diagramma*. Carefully she rearranged the rune into a hieroglyph, a leering pictogram of a jackal.

Then, offering up a silent prayer, she stepped over the line and took the broken body of the adept in her arms.

Estevez had warned her that there was a death bound up in that diagram, and she could distantly hear his shout of denial now.

Helena's body seemed to exhale, a quiet sigh or sob. Then there was the sound of water rushing downhill and Helena's skin sloughed to the floor all around Antigone. Her bones, no longer bound by either the cruel barbed chains of the astors, nor by the more familiar limitations of ligament, followed. They pattered down around Antigone with a musical percussion.

Antigone found herself holding only a tangle of long black robes, a shed skin.

It was the sound of Estevez's voice directly behind her that brought her back from her recollections of her friend and mentor.

"That," he said, "was an extremely foolish thing to do. You know, of course, that you will never leave that circle alive?"

Antigone was calm. She faced him squarely and nodded.

His voice fell to a whisper. "You are a marvel, Antigone. Good bye then, novitia. When you see Helena again, tell her that I did what I could."

"I know you did," she replied, smiling. "You're still a bastard. Sorry I didn't kill you," she added as an afterthought.

His gaze traveled to the gun still clutched in her hand and he raised an eyebrow inquiringly.

"Not that sorry," she said. "I guess you're the one stuck with the astors."

"A temporary inconvenience."

"And Felton and Charlie? You'll let them go. You won't try to track them down?"

"To track them down? Oh, I see. Well, I suppose if they have the good sense to stay out of town. Or perhaps if they were to have a change of heart and consider a new benefactor..."

Antigone snorted. "Oh, that would be precious." She paused. "You'd better go now, before the astors get here."

"I was just going to suggest the same thing to you. Good bye, novitia."

"Good bye, then."

Antigone stepped across the line of the circle, and the death, which had been frustrated and put off overlong, came for her at last. In the empty hall, the report of the pistol rang out a third and final time, more an announcement of her passing than its actual cause.

Chapter Thirty-One
A Messenger

There was a hesitant knock on the imposing steel door of the regent's sanctum. Under normal circumstances, the occupants of the room would have been hard pressed to hear even a battering ram pounding upon the three-foot-thick vault door. The intimidating portal, however, currently stood ajar, a concession to the straggling line of novices that bore the last of the crates into the hall of audience for transport back to the Fatherhouse.

At the rapping, Himes peered up through thick antique spectacles at the novice who wavered on the threshold. The astor had interviewed all of the residents of the chantry during his brief stay here, but for some reason the name of this one escaped him.

Himes raised a finger for his partner to excuse him and made his way over to the novice. "Yes?"

"You said that we were to send for you immediately. If anything should happen, I mean, sir." He shuffled uncomfortably from foot to foot. The novice's timid manner belied his hulking frame, easily six feet tall and almost as broad at the shoulder. On him, the loose black novice robes had something suggestive of a tent about them.

"And something… has happened?" Himes prompted.

"Yes," the novice agreed eagerly, but then his face fell. "But it's not my fault. I wouldn't want you to think that any of this was my..."

"Please do go on," Himes said with a tone of ill-concealed impatience.

"It's just that, I wasn't sure I should come at all, sir. I'd like to say that I ran all the way here, but to tell the truth, I didn't know how you'd take it. Twice I thought better of it and turned back around the way I'd come."

Himes had some slight experience of dissemblers. He cut right to the heart of the matter. "I sense your news is not good. If you deliver it quickly and honestly, you may still escape misfortune. Assuming, of course, that you have had no hand in this mischief yourself."

"No! Of course not, sir. The others, they wouldn't come, said I was crazy for even considering it. But then I thought, they'll be sorry once you do find out. And better you should hear it from me than for me to sit around worrying about what you'd heard."

"Yes, yes. You were quite right to come straight away. Now, what is it that you so desperately want, or don't want, to report?"

"And you promise that, since I myself didn't do the deed— or even see who might have done it—that I won't be sorry for having told you?"

"I have already said so. Now, as neither of us seems to be looking forward to your news, speak now that we might soon move on to some more pleasant diversion."

"Well, it's like this. You know that body, the one you hung in the entry hall and forbade anyone to touch, on pain of death? Well, it's gone," he finished miserably.

"Gone?! How can that be? Now I recall your face. You are one of those idle novices set to keep watch over the adept. Tell me quickly who has done this thing if you wish to keep your own name out of this affair."

The novice looked more terrified and miserable than ever. "I'm sorry sir, but I don't know who is responsible. Her bonds aren't broken, and the protective circle that you inscribed there, it's still intact. And no one could have gotten in or out without our seeing him. Much less so carting a body."

"Is there a problem, Mr. Himes?" Stephens, having stolen silently up behind them, craned over Himes' shoulder. His soothing tone of voice and solemn manner put Himes in mind of a funeral director.

The novice jumped at his sudden appearance and blurted out, "It's a complete mystery, sir. Dead bodies don't just up and disappear." Then, with less conviction and a hint of bitterness, he added, "Not properly dead ones, anyway."

"What?! Surely you don't mean…" He turned his attention on Himes. "You are not talking about Helena," he demanded, daring his fellow astor to contradict him.

"I'm afraid," Himes replied, "that is precisely what this good man is talking about."

Stephens wheeled on the novice, whose trepidation had given way to full-blown panic.

"Please, sirs," he pleaded, looking from one to the other in turn for any sign of support. "When Margot first showed it to us, we were all dumbstruck. We—"

"Well, you are half right," Stephens snapped. "And no one saw who did this thing. An entire gaggle of novices, standing around gawking, and no one to say even how it had been accomplished?"

"No, sir. I mean, that's right, sir. Oh, the accusations flew fast and free among us, each blaming the others while denying any knowledge of the deed whatsoever. It might have come to blows, and would have if there were any doubts as to which of us would come out the better for the scuffle. But there's not one in that whole sorry lot of them I haven't whupped before, and I'm not too shy to say it plainly."

"In the light of the present difficulties," Himes suggested gently, "you might spare us further tales of your athletic prowess. You say all affirm that they saw nothing, heard nothing?"

"I do. And they will say so themselves."

"And you will swear to this, even taking up red-hot iron in your hands and swearing upon it in the ancient way?"

The novice blanched, but squeaked, "If that is what is necessary to convince you, then I'm sure all will so swear. We saw nothing and, if you ask me, there was never anything to see."

At this, Stephens lost patience, "What exactly are you suggesting, then? Ghosts? Supernatural forces? Alien abduction?!"

The novice did not meet his eye. "With all due respect, sir, some of the other novices were saying how it was wrong to try to make it so that she couldn't move on. Unnatural, they said. You can hold back the ravages of death and time only so long, sir, before they come for their own."

"Nonsense," Stephens snapped. "I'm going to the grand foyer and question the other *dumbstruck* novices. Mr. Himes, if you would prepare your deposition iron and join me? Excellent. And as for you..."

He wheeled sharply upon the novice, only to catch sight of the trailing edge of a dark robe vanishing around the corner.

"These foolish whisperings," he said to Himes. "They must be suppressed. Have you ever heard such rubbish? Why, next they will be saying that the saints in heaven came down to gather her in. As if there could be any reason for the greater powers, whether divine or infernal, to so honor her miserable corpse with their attention. Do they think it such an accomplishment to betray one's regent? Do the gods so honor the wicked?"

"Why, then," Himes suggested mildly, "go to all the trouble to deny her a proper death and interment in the first place? Do not mistake me. I'm not for one moment giving credence to these wild speculations. But you must admit that, by the unorthodox sentence you handed down upon the adept, you clearly invited such questions."

"Are you suggesting that all of this is somehow my fault?!"

Himes gestured for Stephens to calm himself. "Nothing of the sort. I am saying only that you have stoked the imagination of the novices with your poetic notions of justice."

Stephens snorted. "Mark my words, when we get to the bottom of this—and we will get to the bottom of it!—what we will find is this defiance has been bought, purchased with the coin of misplaced affections. There is a certain luster to gold that it only gains when clenched tightly in mortal hands. Ideas like loyalty, friendship, love, they have the same mystic luster when they cross the palms of the undying. The allure is just as tantalizing, just as deadly, just as illusory. It is some such romantic notion that has prompted this act. I am certain of it."

"And I am equally certain," Himes said, "that it is some more mundane currency that has tempted our faithful guards to look away at just the right moment."

"Well, that hypothesis should be easy enough to test. In the meanwhile, I will put it to these would-be guards that they will be held personally responsible for the crime. Until such a point, of course, as they produce the real culprit. Are you coming, Mr. Himes?"

"I will gather my things and join you presently."

Chapter Thirty-Two
The Lair of the Jackal

Antigone awoke floating facedown in icy water. Her first reaction was to gasp for air, which was neither necessary nor at all helpful. She sputtered and kicked and eventually managed to get herself upright and treading water.

She broke the surface to find herself in a familiar subterranean pool. She could hear the lapping of water against marble. The obelisks that bordered this hidden chamber were of carved stone. Their markings were clearly of an older order, hieroglyphs both ancient and authentic.

She paddled to the edge of the pool and pushed herself up. Water streamed from her lithe form as she walked dripping from the silent waters. The marble was cool against the soles of her feet.

She expected to be immediately set upon by a vast press of bodies, all clamoring for attention, for vindication, at the water's edge. The area around the Pool of Suicides was always crammed with those still in denial, still clinging to the remains of the lives they had turned their backs upon. But now she saw only a solitary figure in the gloom.

"You have returned to us again, little bird," the Jackal said. He extended a huge onyx-furred hand towards her. His smile was the only light in the chamber. "Done running?"

"Done running," she agreed.

"You have done us a great service, by returning our sister to us. You have honored your dead. For that you have our thanks."

"I didn't do it for you," she said.

"That doesn't matter. You did it for your friend. That does."

"I'm afraid you were right," Antigone said. "I didn't fare any better with the judgment of my own people than I did with your golden scales."

"You could not have," he said. "It was a fool's wager. My scales, at least, have the advantage of being impartial. They do not want anything from you. Your other judges were under no such restriction."

"I think I am ready to face your Devourer now."

"As you wish, little one."

In silence, he led her down the long dark corridor to the Hall of Judgment. A dim red light gleamed on burnished gold, picking out the set of standing scales at the room's focal point.

"Here we are," he said. "I shall adjust the balances. I won't be a moment."

"That won't be necessary." She walked up to the balances and peered in. On one side was a fragile earthen vessel, a canopic jar. On the other a single black feather.

The scales listed dangerously to one side, the weight of the feather raising the jar aloft.

"A good time to die," she said, sizing up the favorable verdict.

"Yes, little one. A good time to die."

About the Author

Eric Griffin is the author of the Tremere Trilogy (*Widow's Walk, Widow's Weeds, Widow's Might*) as well as the novels *Tremere* and *Tzimisce* in the original Clan Novel series.

He is currently co-developer of the Tribe Novel series for **Werewolf: The Apocalypse**. His work on this series includes *Get of Fenris, Fianna, Glass Walkers* and *Black Spiral Dancers*.

His short stories have appeared in the *Clan Novel: Anthology, The Beast Within, Werewolf: The Apocalypse* and *Inherit the Earth*.

Griffin was initiated into the bardic mysteries at their very source, Cork, Ireland. He is currently engaged in that most ancient of Irish literary traditions—that of the writer in exile. He resides in Atlanta, Georgia, with his lovely wife Victoria and his three sons, heroes-in-training all.

Curious about other Crossroad Press books? Stop by our
website: http://crossroadpress.com
We offer quality writing
in digital, audio, and print formats.

Subscribe to our newsletter on the website homepage and
receive a free eBook.